Atheism and Illusion
Richard Dawkins, Derren Brown and God

Mathew Taylor

1. Introduction

General Ignorance

Life is like a magic show. Some people are happy simply to be entertained by it; others want to understand how it's done. The problem though, for those of us in the second category, is that it seems difficult nowadays to understand anything at all. "Thomas Edison stated that we know less than one millionth of 1 percent about anything; Mark Twain thought it would take eight million years to master mathematics alone." This is written on the inside cover of *The Book of General Ignorance* (based on the popular television quiz show *QI*, hosted by Stephen Fry) that I bought this morning from Waterstones in Stratford-Upon-Avon. It is 29th December 2006 and ignorance seems to be becoming very fashionable among the intelligent. In the foreword, Stephen Fry comments on the fact that people often accuse him of knowing a lot. This is what he has to say.

> "This is a bit like telling a person who has a few grains of sand clinging to him that he owns much sand. When you consider the vast amount of sand there is in the world such a person is, to all intents and purposes, sandless. We are all sandless. We are all ignorant. There are beaches and deserts and dunes of knowledge whose existence we have never even guessed at, let alone visited."[1]

He goes on to warn us about people 'who think they know what there is to be known' and think that everything can be explained in a particular book that they may happen to endorse.

> "We are perhaps now more in danger of thinking we know everything than we were even in those dark days of religious superstition (if indeed they have gone away)."[2]

5

Of course, we can trace this idea of ignorance back at least as far as Socrates, who famously claimed to know nothing apart from the fact that he knew nothing. However, among all the general ignorance in which we find ourselves hopelessly lost, there seems to be at least one thing of which we can be absolutely sure. There is no God. If you're not sure about this you need look no further than the Christmas 2006 edition of the *Radio Times* and their exclusive interview with Ricky Gervais, who ends with this advice.

> "Enjoy your days off with the families, sharing gifts and sharing goodwill. But remember, there is no God."[3]

There you go. It's as simple as that. If you don't believe Ricky Gervais, why not read Richard Dawkins' bestselling book *The God Delusion* or Derren Brown's bestselling book *Tricks of the Mind* (in which you will be advised to go and read Richard Dawkins' book). Atheism is a thing to be proud of these days. Not only is it cool, it is logical and it is above all else 'reasonable'. In fact, according to Richard Dawkins, if Jesus were to be born today, even he 'in the light of modern scientific knowledge' would 'see through supernaturalist obscurantism' and, in all likelihood, become an atheist.[4]

Richard Dawkins and Derren Brown

It was in that same branch of Waterstones that, a few months earlier, I first saw the two books that are the reason I am sitting in my study writing this now. These books are *The God Delusion* by Richard Dawkins and *Tricks of the Mind* by Derren Brown. These books will always be very closely linked in my mind for several reasons. I discovered both books for the first time on the same day. I noticed Derren Brown's book first because, for several years, I have been quite a fan of his work. I have read his previous two books[5] and, partly as a result of this, have developed an interest in magic that usually recurs once or twice a year and lasts for several months at a time. (This interest seems to have strong magical powers of its own as, whenever it returns, all my money suddenly disappears). Richard Dawkins' book, on the other hand, caught my attention due to the word GOD being emblazoned across the front cover in very big letters. I am, you see, a Christian and books about God interest me very much. You may think, as I mistakenly did, that Derren Brown and Richard Dawkins are very different characters. Derren Brown is a magician, so that means he is basically a professional liar. Richard Dawkins on the other hand is always talking about truth, so you can imagine my surprise when I noticed, on inspecting the back cover of his book, that it contained a quote from (would you believe it?) Derren Brown who had apparently said,

> "This is my favourite book of all time. I hope that those secure and intelligent enough to see the value of questioning their beliefs will be big and strong enough to read this book. It is a heroic and life-changing work."

Now that is quite a recommendation: 'my favourite book' – 'heroic' – 'life-changing' – and these are the words of Derren Brown, a person whom I must admit to having rather a lot of respect for. Added to that, I rather liked the idea of reading a book called *The God Delusion*. I immediately wondered what God thought of it, and if he found it all rather amusing that two thousand years after his most important work had been completed, people were still arguing about whether he actually existed – and even more amusingly, although in reality rather tragically, coming to the conclusion that he didn't.

I didn't have to read very far into Derren Brown's *Tricks of the Mind* before I discovered that this book, within its pages, also mentions *The God Delusion*. On page fifteen he says,

> "The brave or intelligent Christian who is interested in questioning blind faith would be well advised to read Richard Dawkins' book *The God Delusion*."

He goes on to say that he found Dawkins' book 'enormously valuable' but was sad that many Christians would not only not read the book themselves, they would also try to stop other Christians from reading it. He recommends that Christians read *The God Delusion* 'with an eye to strengthening their own belief.'

It should come as no surprise then that I decided (probably as a result of some powerful suggestion from the great 'psychological illusionist'[6]) that I would follow Derren's advice and read *The God Delusion*, with an eye to strengthening my own belief. Richard Dawkins, however, most definitely does not want you to read his book with an eye to strengthening your existing religious beliefs. He says in the Preface to his book,

> "If this book works as I intend, religious readers who open it will be atheists when they put it down!"[7]

His intended reader is anyone who wants to break free from the shackles of religion. My intended reader is any Christian who wants to hold on to their faith in this age of high profile atheism. In fact, I'll say this now just to make it clear; this is very definitely a 'Christian book'. I am not trying to be 'neutral' because I believe that neutrality is an illusion. I will try to be objective, but only in the sense that I believe that the Christian worldview is the only objective worldview. 'Objectivity' is simply God's subjectivity, in that sense. It also needs to be stated clearly that I am most definitely not writing this book in order to give away any of Derren Brown's magical secrets. I may at times offer my own solution as to how something that resembles one of his effects *could* be achieved, but these solutions will very definitely be my own (as you may guess from their generally inferior nature). As a general rule, I will not comment on any effect of Derren's that I do know the actual method behind.

I also need to say something about words. Richard Dawkins holds the belief that the natural world is all that there is, and that anything supernatural, such as spirits, souls, and God, do not exist. I am going to refer to this belief as 'materialism'. Often it is referred to as 'naturalism' or 'philosophical naturalism', but as Richard Dawkins says in *The God Delusion*, the word 'naturalist' (not to be confused with 'naturist') can also refer to people like David Attenborough (who, as far as I know, is not a naturist). I will use the word 'materialism' to avoid this ambiguity and will not use this word to mean anything else. I will use the word 'God' (with a capital G) to refer to the Christian God. Whenever I use the word 'god' (with a lower-case g), I will be referring to some other god.

It may seem strange for somebody like me, essentially a nobody, to write a book about Richard Dawkins, so I will quickly give you my reasons for doing so. First and foremost, I decided to write this book for my own sake, as I thought it might be quite an interesting study and, I must say, it has indeed been very interesting. I did wonder whether I was really qualified to do it, but then a few things occurred to me. Derren Brown says he has a layman's interest in theology. So do I. Richard Dawkins doesn't even believe that theology is a real subject. Then I remembered that Richard Dawkins is almost certainly far more intelligent than I am. The way I see it though is that if Richard Dawkins has written a book about God, then I can write a book about him, since the 'greatness gap' between God and Richard Dawkins must be considerably bigger than the one between Richard Dawkins and myself. Since Richard Dawkins seems to be aiming his arguments mainly at Christianity[8], I will respond only from the viewpoint of Christianity. This is not, however, meant to be a book of Christian apologetics (by which I mean the defence of the Christian faith), and any time I think apologetics need to be referred to I will try to suggest an appropriate book. There are many great apologetic works available that cover all of the issues raised by Derren Brown and Richard Dawkins perfectly well and I do not intend to simply write a bad rehash of any of them. I am just a very ordinary Christian with an interest in God and an interest in magic.

Christianity and Magic

It seems to me that if there is widespread general ignorance about anything at the moment, it is about Christianity. Contrary to popular belief, Christians generally are not people who are afraid of science and think that the Bible tells us everything that we need to, or would like to, know about the world.

A well known Christian speaker named Ken Ham (recently seen being made to appear ignorant on primetime BBC television by another great intellect of our time, Lord Robert Winston[9]) wrote a book with a man named Paul Taylor (recently seen being branded as stupid, along with 44% of the British population, by the science writer Steve Jones, again on BBC television[10]). They say the following.

> "We human beings are very finite creatures – so much so that no matter how much any person knows, there is infinitely more to learn. This means that no matter how much we know, we are still infinitely ignorant."[11]

Doesn't that sound quite a lot like what Stephen Fry was saying? In fact, don't they appear to be saying exactly the same thing? So in what respect is Stephen Fry different to Ken Ham? How can either of them escape from this terrible ignorance?

It all comes down to their view of how we know things, and that has a lot to do with what we believe about God. Ken Ham, like myself, is very sure that God exists, whereas Richard Dawkins, like Derren Brown, is very sure that he doesn't. Stephen Fry, in his autobiography published in 1997, seemed to be somewhere in between when he made this comment in relation to his being sent away to boarding school at the age of seven.

> "The rightness or wrongness of private boarding education is a separate issue and I change my opinion about it as regularly as I change my socks, the desktop pattern on my computer screen and my views on God."[12]

The question of God is obviously a very difficult one for most people and it deserves to be taken seriously.

When it comes to magic of the occult variety, Christians, as you probably know, are told to have nothing to do with it. When it comes to magic in the sense of conjuring, it is not so clear. A few years ago, I went to see a Christian magician, the late Pete McCahon, perform at a local venue[13]. I've always, in spite of my interest in it, been very slightly dubious about whether Christians should perform magic at all, since it is clearly a form of deception. However, after a considerable amount of thought on the subject (probably far more than was actually required) I came to the conclusion that to 'deceive somebody' with a magic trick, for entertainment purposes, is really no different to 'lying to someone' in the process of telling a joke. Usually the person you are telling the joke to doesn't believe that a *real* man walked into a *real* bar any more than they believe you have real magical powers. With magic tricks as with jokes, it is clear from the way the material is presented that you are not deliberately trying to deceive your audience. Similarly, when Jesus told parables, like the Good Samaritan, it was almost certainly not meant to refer to a real person from Samaria, and his followers would have understood this.

I have wondered sometimes whether the devil, whom the Bible says is a master of deception, ever uses methods similar to those used by professional magicians (for example, Derren Brown; another master of deception) in order to deceive people. If he did, how might he do this? It seems to me that one of the ways in which the devil might try to deceive people could be by having an active role in the production of books such as *The God Delusion*. If the devil were to use methods similar to those of professional magicians, should it therefore be possible to detect methods similar to those used by Derren Brown in a book written by Richard Dawkins? Now, let me make it perfectly clear that I'm not suggesting for a moment that Richard Dawkins is in league with Satan or anything as ridiculous as that. I believe that Richard Dawkins is almost certainly a genuinely honest man who is trying to do what is right. It's just that I, like many religious people, happen to believe that he is wrong.

This book is divided up in the following way. In this chapter, I am simply attempting to give my reasons for writing this book. Chapter 2, entitled 'Pre-Show Work', attempts to establish a foundation for the main sections of the book by setting out some important ideas. Chapter 3, entitled 'Tricks of the Mind', tries to shed a little light on some of the points made by Derren Brown in the first chapter of his book *Tricks of the Mind*, where he discusses his reasons for giving up Christianity. Chapter 4, 'Sleight of Mind', discusses the various individual methods that can be used to deceive, drawing on examples from both Richard Dawkins and Derren Brown. The fifth chapter of the book is a work of fiction entitled 'A Devil's Commentary'. This is my attempt at explaining how the trick called *The God Delusion* could have been done. It is presented as a monologue by a demon (in a style loosely based on C. S. Lewis's book *The Screwtape Letters*)[14], where the demon, who claims to be the influence behind Richard Dawkins' writing of *The God Delusion*, explains his thinking, in a similar way to how a magician would explain the methods behind their magical effects in a book written for the magical community or a DVD commentary. This section is meant to be read side by side with *The God Delusion*. The final chapter 'The Greatest Trick?' attempts to tie things all together and put them into some sort of perspective.

To borrow a term from Richard Dawkins, I intend for this book to be a 'consciousness raiser'. Christians need to be made aware of the deceptive techniques that are used in books like *The God Delusion*. Any time anybody reads Dawkins' book, spiritual warfare will be taking place, and no matter how good or bad the book is, it should be considered dangerous. Harvard psychologist Daniel Gilbert has shown what every politician knows at election time, which is that even when you read something about somebody knowing it to be false, you cannot avoid being influenced by it. This means that when a Christian reads in *The God Delusion* that God is an unpleasant, fictional, petty, unjust, unforgiving control-freak, even though they know it is untrue, they will to some degree be influenced by it. Richard Dawkins knows this, and you can bet Derren Brown knows it too. So is there really anything in common between what these two people have to say? I believe that there is, and over the course of this book I aim to demonstrate why I believe this. I hope you find some of what I have to say interesting. You may not agree with everything (or anything) that I say, but I hope at least that I will provide you with plenty to think about.

2. Pre-Show Work

Presuppositions

When we enter into or try to analyse any situation, we take certain beliefs with us that we already accept as being true. Sometimes we have good reasons for believing these things and sometimes we don't. Either way, we call these beliefs presuppositions. In this section I want to briefly discuss presuppositions and the effect that they have on us. We will look at how they affect our view of history, by considering whether Jesus could simply have been a great magician. Then we will look at how our presuppositions determine how we interpret evidence that can be interpreted in more than one way. After that, I want us to consider another factor that determines how we interpret evidence, namely our will, and how this can seal us into a worldview from which it is very difficult to escape. We will then look at how this is the case for Richard Dawkins' brand of science, and finally consider possible ways of breaking free from these kinds of thinking traps.

Was Jesus Just a Great Magician?

I have an interest in magic and recently performed a trick for a friend of mine. He gave the impression of being quite impressed by it (probably out of kindness) and that was that. Later, I was discussing Christianity with him and he asked the question, "How do we know that Jesus wasn't just a great magician that fooled everyone into thinking he was something that he wasn't?" It seems like a good question. There have been quite a few magic programmes on television recently with titles such as *The Miracles of Jesus* and most recently, over the last few weeks, *Magic Tricks from the Old Testament*. If people can perform similar tricks to Jesus, how do we know we Christians aren't just being duped?

A preacher I heard speak recently put it this way. It is quite a common theory that 'all the miracles were just clever magic tricks and Jesus deceived people into thinking he was someone great'. Of course, people in the first century were far more gullible than us and over the years after he died, Jesus' legend grew until he eventually became known as the Son of God. This sort of argument is often used by unbelievers who are looking for a convenient way of dismissing Jesus, and it fits in very nicely with our very poor understanding of the first century. In reality, magic was a big part of the ancient world. Magicians were everywhere. Nowadays, when we think of magicians we usually think of them as entertainment. In the first century, magicians weren't entertainment. They were sorcerers who were thought to be able to manipulate the divine powers for their own purposes, and they were not always easy to dismiss because they appeared to get results. People were often healed or cursed by them and because of this the authorities, particularly the Jewish authorities, didn't like them at all. When we consider the idea that Jesus may have been a magician, we might be tempted to think that this idea would never have occurred to the people at the time, whereas in reality it would actually have been the first thing that occurred to them. What we really need to ask then is why were the people at the time so convinced that he wasn't a magician, or possibly, if they did suspect that he was a magician, why did this magician get such a following compared to other magicians? There were so many sorcerers around at the time, what made Jesus different? If we read the New Testament carefully, we can see that one of the things it is doing is showing us very clearly that Jesus was not just a magician. Sorcerers at the time used to use very long incantations in order to bring about their cursings or blessings. They also used all sorts of potions, and we have many examples in ancient history of these people doing just this. Jesus was very different. Jesus almost always healed people instantly, by a word, and almost always without any other equipment. He is, to the writers of the New Testament, anything but a sorcerer. We should also remember that sorcery is forbidden by the Old Testament, and if we know anything at all about Jesus, it is that he was very keen on following everything that was written in the Old Testament. But then if Jesus wasn't a sorcerer, who or what was he?

One of the problems with this question is that it is very easy to presume too much about what life in the first century was really like. We presuppose that these people must have been far less astute than we are, when really they almost certainly were not.

What Does a Card Trick Presuppose?

Have you ever wondered what presuppositions we take with us to a card trick? It really depends on the particular trick, but let's look at an example.

Let us say I wanted to perform a simple card trick that went something like this. I place a deck of cards face down on the table and ask you to cut the deck anywhere you choose, very fairly, making two smaller piles of cards on the table, one being what was originally the top part of the deck and the other what was originally the bottom part. I then, using my magical powers, correctly name the card that you cut to. With that, the trick is over and you are suitably a little impressed and more than a little puzzled at how I could possibly have known which card you had cut to.

Anybody who knows anything about magical methods could probably come up with several ways that this simple effect could be achieved. I will suggest four ways that seem to me to be the most obvious. Firstly, it could be that the whole deck is made up of the same card. If the deck contained fifty-two cards that were all the three of spades, then I shouldn't find it too difficult to guess that the card you cut to was the three of spades. A second method could be that the cards have backs that are all secretly marked, enabling me to tell what card has been cut to simply by looking at the back of it. A third method could be that the cards are all stacked in some pre-arranged order. By glimpsing the card above it when the deck is cut, I should be able to accurately name the next card down in the stack. A fourth, slightly trickier, method is that the cards have been tampered with in such a way that when you cut the deck, you will naturally cut them at a particular place.

All of these methods, however, rely on one presupposition; namely that when I originally place the deck face down onto the table, what I have placed on the table is an *ordinary* deck of cards. Unless you believe, usually without directly thinking about it, that I am using an ordinary deck, you will not be particularly surprised when I name the card you have cut to. The presupposition is that the deck is ordinary *and it is our presuppositions that will determine how we interpret the evidence.* The presupposition that I was using an ordinary deck of cards will cause you to interpret what happened as a 'magical' event. That is why it is so bad when a magician starts a card trick such as this by saying something like, "Here I have an ordinary deck of cards." If that had not been said, but simply implied, the participant would probably never have suspected anything else and simply assumed this to be the case.

Now most people that are shown a magic trick do not go away believing that the magician has supernatural powers, usually because (as in the case of Derren Brown) the magician makes it very clear that they don't, but sometimes people do attribute such powers to performers. Allegedly fraudulent mediums have this effect on people all the time. Take, for example, Derek Acorah from television's *Most Haunted* programme. So the story goes, he was recently exposed as a fraud by the makers of the programme[1], yet I know several people who still believe that he has genuine psychic powers. Maybe you know of people who have read about how he was allegedly exposed as a fraud and yet still believe in him. Again, in the case of *Most Haunted*, what we were always shown on television was evidence that could be interpreted in several different ways. In one episode we saw a spoon fly across the room, narrowly missing Yvette Fielding's head. The only problem was that it was thrown from out of shot so we didn't know if it had been thrown by one of the crew or by a genuine ghost. People who are sceptical about the supernatural (for example, Richard Dawkins) would obviously have said that a member of the crew had thrown it, because a disbelief in the supernatural is one of his presuppositions. Others, who want to believe in the spirit world as presented by the likes of Derek Acorah, would be inclined to believe that, quite possibly, it had been thrown by a ghost, particularly as all the crew had sworn that they hadn't touched it. Others, like myself, who do believe in God and the supernatural but suspect that they would probably not want to communicate with us by throwing spoons at us, would side with Richard Dawkins on this one, but for different reasons. It all depends on your presuppositions.

With regard to the card trick I described, the deck is not ordinary in any of the methods I outlined. If it were ordinary in the strict sense of being fifty-two cards that are all different, in no particular order, and not marked or tampered with in any way, I almost certainly would not be able to guess which card you had cut to. As a magician, when I place a deck of cards on the table, I rely on your assumption that the deck is ordinary in order to be able to perform the trick.

Optical Illusions

Optical illusions are often pictures that can be interpreted in more than one way. The Necker Cube is an optical illusion named after the Swiss crystallographer Louis Albert Necker, who first published it in 1832. It is an ambiguous line drawing which can be interpreted in two different ways because whenever two lines cross, the picture does not show which is in front and which is behind[2]. If you stare at the picture, it will often seem to flip back and forth between the two valid interpretations.

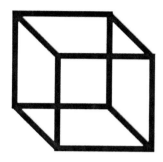

Several years ago, I took a non-Christian friend, who happened to be a professional musician, to a large, evangelical rally that was taking place in the grounds of a nearby stately home. The meeting started, as these kinds of events usually do, with a time of singing. The songs were a mixture of traditional hymns and modern Christian choruses. This was followed by a sermon on one of the Ten Commandments by a fairly well-known local preacher. Towards the end of the sermon, the preacher did what is often referred to as an altar call. This, for anyone who doesn't know, is where the preacher invites anybody who would like to respond to the Christian message to walk down to the front of the hall where they can pray together with a more experienced Christian. My friend watched all of this with a kind of detached curiosity.

After the meeting was over, I asked him what he thought of it all. What he said rather surprised me. Instead of commenting on the content of the sermon, he seemed preoccupied with the music that had preceded it. He said that the music had been written very cleverly, since he knew that music could influence the mood of the listener and make them more receptive to certain kinds of messages. He felt that the congregation had been unwittingly manipulated by the musicians, although he, being aware of the techniques involved, had been able to avoid this, and had remained unaffected by the message that followed the music.

I thought about this for a while and about the interpretation my friend had given to what had gone on. I am well aware that music can affect your mood. I mean, isn't everybody aware of this? The way I see it, God created us. He also created music. He also created our minds to respond in certain ways to certain types of music. If the music that was played put us in a suitable mood for worshiping God, then surely the band were playing perfectly appropriate music. If the music made us more open to the message that was to follow, then surely this was a good thing, as we needed to be made open to the message as there is a part of all of us, even in Christians, that will resist the word of God. We need all the help we can get to overcome these tendencies. I wasn't being manipulated. Music was simply being used for the purpose it was created, as an aid to worshiping God.

What we have here is a sort of Necker Cube effect. The situation is open to two different interpretations. If you think about it, it should be fairly obvious to see the points of view of both myself and of my friend, and often when, as a Christian, I find myself doubting my faith, I feel myself reacting to situations like this in the same way as my brain reacts to the Necker Cube. It sort of flips back and forth from one interpretation to the other. So how do we know which interpretation is true? In the case of the Necker Cube, neither is true. It is deliberately ambiguous, but in the case of what was happening in the meeting surely the answer is simply *if you presuppose Christianity is true*, then you will think my interpretation is correct. *If you presuppose Christianity is not true*, then you will think my friend's interpretation is correct. Now, whether Christianity is true or not will be, before the meeting starts, a presupposition that both of us carry in with us, like the fact that the magician will be using an ordinary deck of cards. For my friend, who entered the meeting not believing in Christianity, to have responded positively to the Christian message would have required him to have been convinced by something else within the message that his presupposed unbelief was mistaken. Unless his presupposition that 'Christianity is false' was changed into a belief that 'Christianity is true' by something within the meeting, he would be destined to leave the meeting, as he in fact did, feeling as though he had successfully avoided an attempt to manipulate him, and in order to discover which interpretation of the meeting is true, what may be required is more evidence.

It is also true in science that presuppositions determine how evidence is interpreted. Here is an example of a scientist making this point.

> "it is not difficult to produce examples from the practice of science that illustrate the same point, namely, that what observers see, the subjective experiences that they undergo, when viewing an object or scene is not determined solely by the images on their retinas but depends also on the experience, knowledge, expectations and general inner state of the observer."[3]

Take the Grand Canyon, for instance, as an extreme example. Many evolutionary geologists believe that the canyon was formed very slowly by the Colorado River. Creationists believe it was formed very quickly by the violent waters of Noah's flood. Ken Ham, the creationist, makes this comment about the Grand Canyon

> "When an evolutionist looks at the Grand Canyon what he sees is something created by a little bit of water and a lot of time. When a creationist looks at the Grand Canyon what he sees is something created by a lot of water and a little bit of time."[4]

Who is right? The problem is that the evidence is open to more than one interpretation and, in the same way, it has often been said that the whole 'book of nature' can be interpreted either theistically or atheistically. It all depends on how you approach it.

It is important to realise that the Necker Cube is an analogy of how the world *appears to be*, and not an analogy of how the world *really is*. Unlike the two interpretations of the Necker Cube which are both valid, the theistic and atheistic worldviews cannot both be true because, simply by the Law of Non-contradiction, A and Not-A cannot both be true at the same time in the same way. God cannot both exist and not exist. So how do we decide which interpretation of the world is the correct one? Surely we need to know more in order to decide which interpretation is right and which is wrong. Surely we need more evidence. But how much evidence is enough? Do you sometimes get the feeling with some people that no amount of evidence would ever be enough? Do you sometimes feel that there must be something going on somewhere that you are not aware of? If you do, then read on, and I'll tell you what all this has to do with Derren Brown.

Invisible Compromise

In his book *Pure Effect*, Derren Brown writes about an idea he calls 'invisible compromise'. I will explain it using an example from one of his television programmes.

In one of his early specials, Derren did a series of effects in a casino. One of them involved him shuffling a deck of cards and then asking a member of the casino staff to call out the name of a card (she called out the nine of clubs, not that it matters). Derren then reached down and cut the deck exactly at the nine of clubs. It was a great trick.

I had a little think afterwards to try to work out how he did it. On the DVD commentary he dismisses it as purely the result of spending far too much time as a youth playing with cards. I, in turn, dismissed this as the usual pseudo-explanation that often accompanies his tricks; I mean, exactly how long would you have to play with cards before you developed the skill of being able to cut to any named card in a shuffled deck? A few false cuts may give the impression to the casino staff that the deck was shuffled but still, how do you cut to any card named at random even from a stacked deck? No matter how many times I watched the clip there was nothing that gave away the method, but obviously something must have been going on. This is what Derren Brown calls invisible compromise. Allow me to explain further.

I asked myself how, if I ever wanted to perform something like this, could I make it look as though I had just cut to a randomly selected card? This is the method I came up with. Let me say at the outset that I don't know how Derren actually did it (which is a good thing because if I don't know the secrets, I can't give them away). Anybody could come up with something like the following method, so I don't feel as though I am saying something that I shouldn't. This is technically *my* method, even if it uses one of Derren Brown's ideas.

I'll start by suggesting some not so good methods. If, instead of asking someone to just call out the name of a card, I ask them to write the name of a card down and then I show them doing this on television, or perhaps I show them choosing a card from another deck, before cutting to exactly the same card, these would be examples of what Derren calls 'visible compromise'. Anybody who was watching, although they wouldn't know exactly what I had done, would suspect that maybe I managed to glimpse what they had written, perhaps using some kind of impression device, or maybe I forced a card on them somehow. They are visible compromises because the audience sees that I am doing something suspicious. The trick is not as 'clean' as if I had just asked them to name a card. But of course no trick is as clean as it appears. There is always a hidden method – a compromise – but a good magician will try to hide this from the audience. They will try to make it invisible. This is particularly easy to do on television because of the ability to edit what the viewer sees, but it is also possible to do this in a live situation. Some examples of 'invisible compromise' (in other words, methods of achieving the required result that the audience will not be able to see, no matter how many times they re-watch the video) are, Derren Brown says, "pre-show work, transmitter equipment, and the advantages offered by the positioning of spectators on stage."[5]

It is important that, even when the sequence is watched over and over again, there is no possible method visible to the viewer. Here, then, is a suggestion as to how you could perform the effect described above.

Before the show starts, ask the spectator to choose a card. Perhaps you could put it to them like this.

"During the performance, I am going to ask you to select a card. I've done this sort of thing in the past though, and I've found that sometimes, with all the lights and cameras on them, people's minds go blank and so to make it easier for you and to save you from any embarrassment, and also because we can't really afford to do too many takes, I wonder if you'd mind choosing the card you are going to say in advance. It's just not worth taking the risk, I don't think. Actually, in fact, to make it fair, because I know that psychologically many people will actually choose the same cards when asked, just to make sure I don't have any advantage in that way, why don't you just select the card at random from this deck here?"

Then you force a card on them. Doesn't that sound so fair though? It shouldn't be too difficult to cut a stacked (or not) deck at a place you know in advance, should it? And the great thing is that no matter how many times people watch the DVD they won't have a clue how you did it (like I don't know how Derren did it). That's why it's called *invisible* compromise. This is what is known as pre-show work. You can occasionally get some idea that it has gone on if the person involved is not quite as amazed by the trick as you expected them to be; but what does that matter? Nobody else knows. It's still a great trick and Derren Brown is still a great magician.

Now what has all this got to do with Richard Dawkins?

Hermetically Sealed Worldviews

Whenever you enter into a discussion with an atheist, or anybody with a different worldview to your own, it can sometimes be quite amazing how effortlessly they seem to be able to ignore or dismiss arguments that to you seem extremely powerful. It is as if something is going on that you don't know about. What you have in these situations is a classic example of invisible compromise. It is important to realise that before you start talking to somebody like Richard Dawkins, an awful lot of pre-show work has already been done. Let me give you some examples. In his chapter entitled 'Arguments for God's Existence', Dawkins' main argument against Pascal's Wager (simply put, this is Pascal's argument that we should believe in God because it is the most sensible bet) is I think, even by the standards of *The God Delusion*, incredibly simplistic. Dawkins' objection is that he cannot choose to believe something simply as an act of the will.[6] In other words, he can't choose to believe something is true simply because he wants to believe it is true. Compare this with what Blaise Pascal himself said.

> "People almost invariably arrive at their beliefs not on the basis of proof but on the basis of what they find attractive."[7]

Even if we acknowledge that Pascal was possibly exaggerating to make a point, surely we must admit that there is some truth in what he is saying. We have already considered the case of *Most Haunted*'s Derek Acorah. Similarly, after Derren Brown's *Séance* was shown on Channel Four in 2003, psychologist Richard Wiseman, Professor of the Public Understanding of Psychology at the University of Hertfordshire, made this comment about people who attempt to contact the dead via a medium,

"We want to believe that the statement is true, that it applies to us. So we tend to buy into it."[8]

But surely we don't need a professor to tell us this. Isn't it obvious that we are more inclined to believe the things we want to believe? One of the really fascinating things about Christianity is that it is often accepted as truth by people who really, really *don't* want it to be true. C. S. Lewis was a good example of this. Personally, I find it incredible how, as a Christian, when I really want to do something that goes against my faith (as I am often prone to do), the evidence for Christianity starts to become temporarily less convincing, and I start thinking about all the evidence that could be used against my beliefs.

Christianity offers us what I consider to be a very convincing explanation of this phenomenon. The Bible says that we are all living in rebellion against God. Even as Christians there is a part of us that remains in this state until we die. John 3:19 says that men love darkness rather than light because their deeds are evil, and that nobody wants to come into the light for fear that their deeds will be exposed. In other words, we love truth as long as it suits us. If, however, it doesn't suit us then we can easily convince ourselves that a little lie doesn't really matter. Teachings in the Bible such as these just seem to make sense to me. From my point of view, they are good pieces of evidence that point to the authenticity of Christianity as a whole. As a worldview, Christianity seems to have a lot of explanatory power, like a good scientific theory. Of course, these observations are not conclusive proof that Christianity is true, and they are not meant to be but, as I see it, there are just so many things that Christianity seems to explain extremely well.

Here is another example. As far as the question of truth goes, it has always seemed very odd to me why so many atheists seem to value truth so much. It certainly isn't something that naturally follows from Darwinian evolution. Many creatures use deception to aid their survival, so why should we humans suddenly be so devoted to truth? What makes us any different? The Christian view that we are made in God's image and that God is a God of truth seems to me to be far more plausible.

What about good and evil? Here again is something that troubles me when I read *The God Delusion*. Richard Dawkins seems to have a big problem with the concepts of good and evil. This is not surprising as good and evil belong to a theistic worldview and not to an atheistic one. In a Darwinian world, there is no good behaviour and no evil behaviour; there is just behaviour. In a previous book, Dawkins famously stated that the universe has "no design, no purpose, no evil and no good, nothing but blind pitiless indifference." In other words, good and evil, in the sense that these words would naturally be understood by the average reader, do not really exist.[9] In *The God Delusion*, he admits that if they did exist in an 'absolute' way, this would seem to point to the existence of something supernatural[10], but then when he starts to talk about morality having a Darwinian origin, he talks about altruism being beneficial to a gene's survival and gives the example of "being good to one's own children"[11] which, as I'm sure you will have noticed, contains the word 'good', presumably to mean something to an average reader. This seems to me to be, at best, very odd. Dawkins does not here define what he means by 'good'. If you don't believe that 'good' actually exists, then why keep on using the word? Dawkins is very critical of scientists who use the word 'God' in a metaphorical way. I think it would make things a lot clearer if he stopped using the word 'good' and replaced it with something else. If what he means by 'good' is behaviour that will favour the survival of a gene, then why doesn't he say this? Perhaps he doesn't mean this, since this idea does in practice seem a little bit unsatisfactory. For example, I have taken pains in this book, when writing about Derren Brown, not to disclose any of his magical methods (I have already said that I don't know what many of them are, but my attitude would be the same even if I did) because I think it would be morally wrong for me to do so – after all, they are his ideas and if he has chosen not to make them public then neither should I. According to my beliefs, this behaviour would not be 'good'. It would be difficult to argue though that my not giving away Derren Brown's magical methods was 'good' behaviour, if what I meant by 'good' was behaviour that favoured the survival of my genes. I don't know how Richard Dawkins would explain why it was good behaviour to keep Derren Brown's secrets. Also, according to Charles Darwin (and therefore Richard Dawkins), natural selection should eliminate from humanity any traits that are not good for us; by which I mean by 'good' here, traits that hinder our survival. Why is it then that our tendency to believe in God has not been removed by natural selection if it is so bad for us? Richard Dawkins recently made a television programme, called *Root of All Evil?*, saying that belief in God was, to some extent, a cause of evil in the world. Firstly, doesn't it seem strange that included in the title of his programme is the word 'evil' (although Dawkins has said that he did not choose this title himself), in a way that seems to suggest that evil is something he believes in, when he has said before that evil does not exist, or are we not meant to notice this? Also, surely religion can't be evil in the sense that it is bad for the survival of humanity, which seems to be the message of the programme, since if religion is a cause of that kind of 'evil', and natural selection has not weeded it out, then natural selection is not doing its job properly, and in *The God Delusion* Richard Dawkins says that natural selection is able to explain "the whole of life."[12] Also, in *The God Delusion*, Dawkins suggests that religion is an "accidental by-product" of evolution.[13] However, the question must then be asked how do we decide what is an accident? The answer would seem to be that anything not removed by natural selection *that we personally do not like* must be an accidental by-product. This all sounds very suspicious to me. After all, according to Darwinism, isn't everything meant to be accidental?

The truth is that we all want what we want to be true to be the truth, and this applies as much to Richard Dawkins as it does to anybody else. However, the fact that we want something to be true bears no relation whatsoever to whether it is actually true or not.

As Derren Brown says in *Tricks of the Mind*, when we really want something to be true, we don't even bother sometimes to consider the evidence that may disprove the thing we want to believe. We just pretend that the evidence is not there and create what is sometimes referred to as a hermetically sealed worldview. However, it seems to me to be people like Richard Dawkins, not Christians, who are most guilty of this. God is not allowed to be considered as an explanation for anything and must be kept out at all costs. In his book *The Problem of Pain*, the writer and Christian apologist C. S. Lewis famously said that the gates of hell are locked from the inside[14], meaning that all those who are in hell are ultimately there by choice. The same can surely be said of all those people living inside the hermetically sealed worldview of materialistic science.

Another example of invisible compromise can be seen in the following example.

Loaded Dice

The term 'loaded dice' refers to dice that are meant to produce skewed or predictable results, but it can also be used generally to describe a situation where somebody has an unfair advantage. In magic, the performer always has an unfair advantage. This is due to another case of invisible compromise.

Derren Brown is well known for being able to guess which hand somebody is holding a coin in. He claims to do it by reading the person's body language but, however he does it, he never seems to fail. If he does read the person's body language, the trick could be said to be 'fair'. I, however, am not so skilled. Let's say there is a product on the market that is a sort of small metal detector that you can strap to your arm, concealing it beneath your jacket. Not only will it detect a coin in someone's hand, but it can even detect the metallic strip in a bank note, making it possible for you to discern which envelope somebody has hidden it in by 'observing their body language.'[15] If I used such a device, the experiment would not be fair, although to the participant it may present the illusion of fairness. In reality though, the metaphorical dice would be well and truly loaded.

What most people do not realise is that science itself presents a similar loaded dice situation when it comes to the issue of impartiality. If science were impartial to the issue of God, you should be able to carry out an experiment to try to decide scientifically whether or not God exists (if, for the sake of argument, we presume that such an experiment were possible). You should be able to look at the results of your experiment and conclude either yes, I believe from my results that God exists or no, I don't believe that God exists.

Now this is *not* the case in reality because science has a hidden (to many people) presupposition. Science presupposes that a materialistic explanation (one that does not involve God) exists for every situation. Materialism is the belief that the natural world is all that there is, and anything supernatural, such as spirits, souls, and God, are presumed not to exist.

This is how Phillip Johnson, one of the leaders of the Intelligent Design movement, puts it.

> "'science' as defined in our culture has a philosophical bias that needs to be exposed. On the one hand, science is empirical. This means that scientists rely on experiments, observations and calculations to develop theories and test them. On the other hand, contemporary science is naturalistic and materialistic in philosophy. What this means is that materialistic explanations for all phenomena are assumed to exist."[16]

This is clearly the view of Richard Dawkins, as in *The God Delusion* he claims to decry all forms of supernaturalism.[17] He elsewhere writes that

> "Our philosophical commitment to materialism and reductionism is true, but I would prefer to characterise it as a philosophical commitment to a real explanation as opposed to a complete lack of an explanation."[18]

How he prefers to characterise it is neither here nor there. It is what it is. What this means in practice is that no matter how convincing the case for God's existence might be, he is assumed to not exist, by definition, before any experiment has even begun. Any claims, such as those of creationists, that involve God are automatically classed as 'not scientific' because of the invisible compromise of a presupposed materialism. When coupled with the fact that they *don't want* God to exist, it means that any empirically verifiable evidence for God's existence is simply ignored.

The only way to help a person to break free from their hermetically sealed worldview is to try to show them that their beliefs are inconsistent with each other or contain problems that are difficult to resolve. You may then be able to convince them that another worldview, perhaps yours, provides a better explanation of the available evidence and contains less inconsistencies and problems than theirs does. These are part of the function of what Richard Dawkins calls the 'Arguments for God's Existence'. For example, one such problem with materialism can, I think, be illustrated in the following way.

Magic Broomsticks

Richard Dawkins' well-known book *The Blind Watchmaker* was originally published in 1986 and Derren Brown's original television special *Mind Control* first aired in the year 2000. But is the Richard Dawkins who wrote *The God Delusion* the same Richard Dawkins who wrote *The Blind Watchmaker*, and is the Derren Brown who wrote *Tricks of the Mind* the same

Derren Brown who starred in the television special *Mind Control*? Now, before you dismiss me as completely insane for asking these ridiculous questions, I am attempting here to make a serious point. Many atoms in our bodies are replaced every single day. The statistics on this differ slightly depending on the source, but it seems likely that around 98% of the atoms in your body are replaced every year. The way we retain our memories in spite of this process is that, although the atoms in our body are replaced, the structures and their interactions that make our memories remain. It really is a very curious process. Nobel Prize winning physicist Richard Feynman put it this way.

> "So what is this mind of ours: what are these atoms with consciousness? Last week's potatoes! They now can remember what was going on in my mind a year ago – a mind which has long ago been replaced."[19]

So if all, or practically all, of the atoms in Richard Dawkins' body have been replaced many times since 1986, is it fair to say that the Richard Dawkins alive today is the same Richard Dawkins that wrote *The Blind Watchmaker*?[20]

One of the 1996 Christmas episodes of *Only Fools and Horses* was called *Heroes and Villains* (the one where Del and Rodney dress up as Batman and Robin) and it contained a scene in which Trigger (the road sweeper whose purpose it is to make stupid comments) makes this comment about his broom. "I've maintained it for 20 years. This old broom has had 17 new heads and 14 new handles in its time." Another character understandably asks how it can possibly be the same broom. This scene gets a very big laugh because, obviously, it is very funny. (In fact, in 2006, over 35,000 viewers of UKTV Gold voted it the 10th funniest ever *Only Fools and Horses* moment!) It was funny because Trigger is stupid. How can it possibly be considered the same broom if the whole broom has been replaced 14 times in the past 20 years? But then what about Richard Dawkins? Can he possibly be considered to be the same person if the atoms in his body have been replaced many times since 1986? Even if it turned out that the figure I quoted of 98% were higher than the actual amount, what is walking around today and calling itself Richard Dawkins is not the same collection of atoms that wrote *The Blind Watchmaker*. If you want to argue something like it is the structure of Richard Dawkins' brain being maintained that makes him the same person, then that doesn't help. If today's Richard Dawkins is the same person who wrote *The Blind Watchmaker* in 1986 then Trigger is still right because the structure of his broom has remained the same too.

Now, let me give you my opinion. As a Christian I think that the answer is yes, obviously today's Richard Dawkins is the same Richard Dawkins, but I believe this because I believe that humans have souls, and that the soul is the part that defines an individual and it is this that stays the same even though the atoms that make up our bodies change over time. On the other hand, if I were a materialist and believed that all we are is a collection of atoms then surely it's not obvious at all. I mean, was Trigger actually right after all? I'd probably have to, reluctantly, admit that he was, and then ask myself why I found his comment so funny.

I cannot prove, in the way that many atheists such as Richard Dawkins insist that it must be proved, that we have a soul. It is just something that I believe because it seems to make sense of what I experience and it is another example of what I would consider to be good evidence in favour of the Christian worldview. What it comes down to is, as a Christian, I don't believe Trigger was right, so therefore neither do I believe materialists like Richard Dawkins are right, because if I'm on the side of the materialists then I'm on the side of Trigger, and if I find myself laughing at Trigger along with the majority of the western world (including over 35,000 viewers of UKTV Gold), then I am in fact laughing at myself. If I *were* a materialist, little things like this would bother me because, as we all know, Trigger is supposed to be stupid and Richard Dawkins most definitely isn't.

3. Tricks of the Mind

One of the Oldest Tricks in the Book

If we're going to be discussing tricks and magical methods in this book, we may as well look at one of the oldest tricks in the book - according to Richard Dawkins, that is. On his website, dated Saturday 18th November 2006, Dawkins has written an article entitled *I'm an atheist... BUT,* which begins like this.

> "Of all the questions I fielded during the course of my recent book tour, the only ones that really depressed me were those that began "I'm an atheist, BUT . . ." What follows such an opening is nearly always unhelpful, nihilistic or – worse – suffused with a sort of exultant negativity. Notice, by the way, the distinction from another favourite *genre:* "I *used* to be an atheist, but . . ." That is one of the oldest tricks in the book, practised by, among many others, C S Lewis, Alister McGrath and Francis Collins. It is designed to gain street cred before the writer starts on about Jesus, and it is amazing how often it works. Look out for it, and be forewarned."

I was therefore rather amused to notice that this is exactly how Derren Brown begins his book *Tricks of the Mind,* by saying essentially, *"I used to be a Christian, BUT..."* In fact, he devotes several pages to explaining why he gave up Christianity and, in a moment, we will take a look at them

Do As I Do

'Do as I do' is an example of what is called a magical plot, by which magicians mean a particular story or theme that a trick is based upon. Examples of other magical plots could be a torn and restored card, or cutting someone in half and putting them back together again.[1]

Here is an example of a well-known 'do as I do' trick you might like to try with someone – preferably somebody young and naïve. You'll need two decks of cards. Tell your victim that they must do everything that you do. Begin by picking up one of the decks. They pick up the other one. Shuffle your deck. They shuffle the other one. What you must do at this point is notice which card is on the bottom of their shuffled deck. This will be what is called your 'key card.'[2] (Try not to let them see you looking – that would be a visible compromise!) Say that you now want them to pick any card from their face-down deck and place it, still face-down, on top of their deck. (This works better if you can both spread the decks out face down in front of you but it's not really important – it just looks nicer). You say that you will now, in a moment, do the same and pick a card from your deck and this is where the magic happens because you are going to attempt to choose the same card as they did, even though you don't actually know what card they chose. Tell them to think very clearly of their card. Tell them to picture it in their mind. You now search through your deck and take out any card you like at random, saying something like, "Yes, I think I've got the same card as you, but I'm not sure." Place this random card face-down on top of your deck. Now you give your deck a complete cut and they give their deck a complete cut. Now, you say, you need to swap decks. Tell them to look for their card in your deck while you look for your card in their deck. What you actually do is find their card, which will obviously be, because of the cut, the one directly under the key card. When they have found their card, you can finish the trick by showing them that your card is in fact the same card as theirs.

The reason I have referred to the 'do as I do' plotline here is that, the way I see it, when it comes to deciding on why we believe things, in many ways I just do as Derren Brown does. He also does what he would say I do.

Disillusionment

Derren Brown used to be a Christian. In the first chapter of *Tricks of the Mind* he gives us his reasons for abandoning Christianity.[3]

It seems that, as a Christian, Derren Brown was troubled by the following problem. Anybody can be a true believer in anything, but that doesn't make your beliefs true. What separates my firm convictions from other people's firm convictions? This is obviously a real problem, and one that I myself struggled with for a long time. In the end I came to the conclusion that the answer to the question of what separates my firm convictions from other people's firm convictions has to be, and I'm sure Derren Brown and Richard Dawkins would agree, evidence. So if we all agree on this, why am I a Christian when Derren Brown and Richard Dawkins are both atheists? Well, surely it must be at least partly because I think the evidence does support Christianity, whereas Derren Brown and Richard Dawkins don't. So what does Derren Brown actually say about this?

Magic Circularity

He says that believers in the paranormal have a 'circular belief system', by which he says that they ignore any evidence that goes against their beliefs and only take any notice of evidence that supports their beliefs. (In this book I will refer to this kind of reasoning as Magic Circularity, in order to distinguish it from traditional circularity, which is an argument where one or more of its premises presupposes its conclusion.) Now, in classic Derren Brown style, there is obviously some truth in this. None of us can examine all of the evidence available. What we tend to do is to consider some of the available evidence and decide whether it supports or contradicts whatever it is we are testing the believability of. If we find that it does support our beliefs, we look for more evidence. Derren Brown says openly that this is what he himself does.

> "I have a layman's interest in this sort of scholarship, coupled with a personal desire to back up my disbelief in the way I expected I should be able to back up my belief when I had it."[4]

Like everybody else, we want to find things that back up our beliefs. Now if we find something that seems to go against our beliefs, should we immediately discard them? Surely not, and incidentally this is also how science works. We investigate further to find out whether the evidence really does contradict our beliefs or whether there is some other explanation. It may be that we do not see how the evidence fits in with our beliefs even though it actually does. Sometimes we are even prepared to live with an apparent contradiction for a while, on the assumption that eventually, when we know more, it will be resolved.

Now, the point that people sometimes tend to ignore any evidence that goes against their beliefs and only take any notice of evidence that supports their beliefs is very important because Derren Brown is still doing it himself in his book. It's just another case of 'do as I do'. There are many excellent reasons to think that the Bible *is* historically reliable. I will not write down a list of reasons here, as my reason for writing this is not to write a book of Christian apologetics, in the same way that Derren Brown did not list any evidence to support his view that the Bible is not history. Anybody who wants to examine the evidence could probably do no better than starting by reading Norman Geisler and Frank Turek's great book *I Don't Have Enough Faith to be an Atheist*.

Derren Brown is ignoring all of the evidence that does not support his position and concentrating on all of the evidence that does, although I would hope that he is, like myself, not simply *ignoring* the evidence that does not support his position, but rather trying to come up with convincing counter-arguments that explain that evidence.

He suggests that Christians are all guilty of believing "comforting nonsense"[5], but surely for the Christian and the atheist the question should not be *is it comforting?* but rather *is it true?* An atheist serial killer no doubt finds his belief that when he dies he will not have to answer to God equally

37

comforting. Being comforting neither proves nor disproves anything and should not be allowed to cloud the issue. There is a lot about Christianity that I don't find comforting (like the idea that most of my family may be going to hell when they die) but there is also a lot that I do find comforting. C. S. Lewis didn't become a Christian because he found it comforting. This is what he famously said about his conversion.

> "In the Trinity Term of 1929 I gave in, and admitted that God was God, and knelt and prayed: perhaps, that night, the most dejected and reluctant convert in all England."[6]

We are in a very unusual position at the moment, living in the west in the twenty-first century. In many parts of the world today, if you become a Christian, it is quite likely that you will be severely persecuted. This has typically been the case historically all over the world. We can read of many such stories, like the one of Richard Wurmbrand, who spent a total of fourteen years imprisoned under (quite literally) the Communists in Romania.

> "On Sunday, February 29, 1948, Pastor Wurmbrand was on his way to church when he was kidnapped by a small group of secret police. He tells what happened next: 'I was led to a prison thirty feet beneath the earth where I was kept in solitary confinement. For years, I was kept alone in a cell. Never did I see sun, moon, stars, flowers. Never did I see a man except the interrogators who beat and tortured me.'"[7]

Does that sound comforting enough? Currently there are around 150,000 Christians each year who are killed for their faith. That's about 3 every 10 minutes. It really is too easy just to say people become Christians because it is comfortable, because for millions of Christians down through the centuries it has not been in the least bit comfortable.

It must be admitted that there is some truth in the fact that certain aspects of religion do offer us comfort at certain times. Alister McGrath, in his book *Dawkins' God*, mentions that in the course of a debate on *Whether Science is Killing the Soul*, a member of the audience asked Richard Dawkins whether science was able to offer consolation in the way that religion does – for example, after the death of a close friend or relative? This was Dawkins' response.

> "The fact that religion may console you doesn't of course make it true. It's a moot point whether one wishes to be consoled by a falsehood."[8]

McGrath then points out that this is bad logic on the part of Dawkins. It does not logically follow that something is false, simply because it has not been proven. Now I want to stop and ask a question. Is Richard Dawkins stupid? Well, obviously he is most definitely *not* stupid. He is extremely intelligent. So I'll ask another question. Why would an intelligent person like Richard Dawkins give such an odd answer? Logical errors such as this one will be looked at in more detail later in the book.

Derren Brown goes on to say that the New Testament has been edited for political and social reasons over the centuries and that the gospels were not written by the people who claim to have written them. In short, we cannot take the New Testament at face value.[9]

In response to this, Christians can be confident that there is plenty of evidence to suggest that this is not the case. Anybody wanting to read a summary of this evidence could do no better than reading F. F. Bruce's classic book *The New Testament Documents: Are They Reliable?* Having read that, and having been presented with evidence for both sides of the argument, it would be up to you to make a reasoned decision which evidence to accept and which to reject. If however, you are only reading Derren Brown's book, ironically you are doing exactly the thing that Derren Brown, in that very book you are reading, is criticising people for doing, namely only looking at one side of the debate.

Derren Brown says that believers are not encouraged to question their faith. He quotes Richard Dawkins' expression that "any rational inquiry is expected to 'tip-toe respectfully away' once religion enters the room."[10] Now this may sometimes be the case, but it is not always the case, and it is not the case in my experience. To claim that it is the normal Christian attitude is simply a caricature of the Christian faith. As Derren Brown knows, we can be very easily influenced and controlled by other people (after all, that is how he makes his living), therefore it would be silly, never mind immensely tiresome, to continually go out of our way to read more and more books that are persistently challenging our beliefs. In some cases, we may not be able to answer all the objections that may be raised. This does not mean, however, that there are no answers and it most definitely does not mean that we have not been sensible in deciding what we believe to be true.

Derren Brown says that "it is something of an insult to the very truth I might hold dear to say that something is true just because I believe it is."[11] I don't know anybody, Christian or non-Christian (apart from some philosophers), who would say that something is true just because they believe it is. People generally believe things to be true for a reason. He goes on to say that "to decide that the entire universe operates in such and such a way... that should demand a higher level of argument than 'It's true because I really, really feel it is.'"[12] But why might I really, really feel it is true? If it is because I am satisfied that I have considered much of the available evidence, and I have come to the conclusion that the best explanation of the evidence is a theistic explanation, then surely it is absolutely fine to believe in God because I really, really feel that a theistic worldview is true. That is surely the best anybody can do. We cannot have one hundred percent certainty about anything. Richard Dawkins himself says, about his atheism, that he lives his life as an atheist because he thinks God's existence is very improbable. Even he is not certain of this fact.[13] I would simply say the opposite; that I cannot know for certain but I think a theistic worldview best explains the available evidence and I live my life on the assumption that God *is* there. What is wrong with that?

Half Truths

Now we come to the reason Derren Brown gives for abandoning Christianity and I was surprised to discover that I think it contains what I consider to be a very subtle and deceptive half truth. This is what he says.

> "To me and my erstwhile fellow Christians, it all rested on whether or not Christ really came back from really being dead. If he was actually resurrected as it says in the Bible, then it's all true."[14]

> "When I realized that the accounts of Jesus were just tales, I had to accept that the resurrection could not be argued from those very sources as fact, which unavoidably led to the conclusion that nothing separated my 'true belief' from anyone else's 'true belief'."[15]

I think this is misleading for the following reason. Derren says "it all rested on whether or not Christ really came back from really being dead."

The apostle Paul himself said, in 1 Corinthians 15:13-14, that our faith is useless if Jesus has not actually been raised from the dead. In other words, if it can be proved that Jesus was *not* resurrected, then we should give up Christianity. Now obviously it has *not* been proved that Jesus did not rise from the dead. Such a thing *could not* be proved (although at the time of Paul's writing, it arguably could have been), particularly as our most reliable historical documents from the time (namely the New Testament documents) insist that he *did* rise from the dead. It is important to realise that what the apostle Paul is saying is *not* what Derren Brown is saying. Derren Brown is saying that whether Christianity is true or not *all rests on whether Jesus was raised from the dead*. But it doesn't all rest on this at all. Of course a belief in the resurrection is a necessary condition for calling yourself a Christian, as far as most people are concerned, but my faith rests on many other things apart from my belief in the resurrection. When I think carefully about the world, and when I consider what it means to be human, I simply believe that a theistic worldview explains all of the evidence better than an atheistic one; and there is a lot of evidence to support this claim. For example, how did the universe, very finely tuned to support life, arise out of nothing? How do we explain consciousness? How do we explain our sense of morality? How do we explain human dignity and human depravity? How do we explain the countless religious experiences people have claimed to have had? Then we have the testimony of the Bible and the early Christians. Why would they sacrifice themselves for a lie? Oh, I almost forgot (strangely, as Richard Dawkins seems to think that it is the only thing that Christians cling desperately to) how do we explain the 'apparent design' that is everywhere we look? Everybody has to decide whether these facts (and all the others) fit best into a theistic worldview or an atheistic one. Ravi Zacharias, the Christian philosopher, says that any worldview must satisfy three criteria: it must possess logical consistency, empirical adequacy and experiential relevance.[16] I believe that Christianity possesses all three of these.

It is simply not true to suggest that the Christian faith ever simply hangs on just one particular piece of evidence. Richard Dawkins, unlike Derren Brown, does not believe that Christianity hangs on one piece of evidence; he believes it hangs on no evidence at all.[17] I hope it is obvious to you that he can only hold that view if he is either hopelessly ignorant (which I am sure he is not) or if he is using the word 'evidence' in an unusual way. This idea of using words to mean what they do not usually mean is something we will come back to later.

The Illusion of Impartiality

Derren Brown also says that "to decide that the Bible is history, one must ignore the vast amount of impartial biblical research that shows it really isn't."[18]

Now, if there is one thing that seems perfectly clear from experience, it is that biblical research is *never* impartial. People get very emotional about Christianity, for the simple reason that it is just not possible to understand the Christian message and then say that you do not care whether it is true or not. Anybody who thinks it is possible not to care whether Christianity is true or not does not fully understand what it claims. People who do understand what is being said will always have a point of view and will often hold it very strongly. If you need evidence of this, just read the reviews of Christian books on the Internet.

Derren Brown says, "The Bible is not history."[19] One anonymous reviewer of the fairly well-known Christian book, *The Bible as History* by Werner Keller, gave the book only one star on Amazon's website and said that it was "full of outright lies and nonsense", contained "obvious misinterpretations" and set out to prove its hypothesis "by manipulating sketchy evidence." Apparently, this book is only suitable for an individual with "a low level of gullibility." This is hardly an impartial or unemotional review, but it is typical. By the way, shouldn't that be a *high* level of gullibility?

A similar review of a book called *The Dawkins Delusion* by Alister McGrath (written as a response to *The God Delusion*) is worth noting, since it was posted *two months before* the book was actually published. In it the reviewer says it is a book "for anyone confused by Dawkins' clear, succinct reasoning and [sic] wishes to cling to their ancient faith despite all the evidence", and that "the job of theology is to tell the simple minded how to think." He calls Christians "faith junkies" who are "terrified of Dawkins" and seems to be claiming that Alister McGrath only wrote this book for the money. He also gives the book one star, presumably because you can't give it any less. It is interesting, but not necessarily significant, to note that most of these people claim that atheism is the way of the intellectually enlightened thinker, but the reviews themselves often contain appalling spelling and grammar. It is as though Christianity just makes them so angry that they feel that they just have to lash out at it.

Richard Dawkins' website is full of the same sort of thing. In another comment about Alister McGrath's book, *The Dawkins Delusion*, this time three months before the book was published, somebody calling himself 'Andew' gives the opinion that "Prof ALISTer mcgRATh wants to sell his book badly." I presume by this he means that Alister McGrath really wants to sell copies of his book, which I suppose is true. Andew's comment stands out as it is rather amusing. You will of course have noticed how Andew has capitalised certain letters in Alister McGrath's name, in order to brand him an A-LIST RAT for daring to criticise Richard Dawkins (I thought this was actually quite clever). If you are familiar with the many books written by Alister McGrath (who also works at Oxford University alongside Richard Dawkins) you will no doubt be aware that they are of the highest quality, and that Andew seems completely unaware of this, possibly because he only ever reads one side of the argument. Alister McGrath certainly has nothing to prove about himself by writing a book about Richard Dawkins.

The fact is that the Christian gospel is meant to be offensive to unbelievers because it says that they are sinners that will, if they fail to repent and trust in Christ, eventually go to hell. You cannot be impartial about this and you either believe it or you don't. You get a sense of the emotion aroused by this in Dawkins all the time. Listen to the way he refers to God.

> "The God of the Old Testament is arguably the most unpleasant character in all fiction: jealous and proud of it; a petty, unjust unforgiving control-freak; a vindictive, bloodthirsty ethnic cleanser; a misogynistic, homophobic, racist, infanticidal, genocidal, filicidal, pestilential, megalomaniacal, sadomasochistic, capriciously malevolent bully."[20]

Surely nothing more needs to be said.

Not Enough Evidence

The philosopher and atheist Bertrand Russell famously said that if, when he died, he found out that God actually did exist, he would complain that there had not been enough evidence for his existence. In an interview with *The Guardian* newspaper, dated 10th January 2006, Richard Dawkins said the same thing.

> "And what if, by some mischance, he were to find there is a God when he dies? He looks at me as if I were mad. "The question is so preposterous that I can hardly grace it with a hypothetical answer," he says finally. "But, to quote Bertrand Russell, I suspect I would say, 'There's not enough evidence, God'.""

Richard Dawkins has previously said, in *The Blind Watchmaker*, that if he had lived before 1859, the year Charles Darwin's *The Origin of Species* was published, he would not have been an atheist. He simply says

> "I could not imagine being an atheist at any time before 1859"[21]

Presumably then, before Darwin, there *was* enough evidence to make belief in God reasonable (or is Richard Dawkins saying that before 1859 he would not have based his beliefs on evidence? I don't think he is saying that.) So what has changed since Darwin? Is there less evidence for a belief in

God now than there was in 1858? Well, surely the answer has to be no. All the evidence that was there in 1858 is still there. It also has to be said that we have a lot more evidence now that seems to point to the existence of a Creator than we had in 1858. For example if you subscribe to the Big Bang theory, which wasn't around then, you have to explain how something came out of nothing (before this you could say, like Bertrand Russell said, that the universe has always been "just there"). How did life arise from non-living matter? How did conscious minds come out of mindless matter? We also know now about the hundreds of so-called anthropic constants, which are all the ways in which the universe seems to have been very finely tuned in order to be able to support human life.[22] On top of that we have much better versions of all the classic philosophical arguments for God and better archaeological evidence to support the Bible. I'm sure that Richard Dawkins would point to new evidence that seems to support his point of view too, but what we need to understand is that since Darwin, the primary thing that has changed is not the available evidence. What changed is that Darwin provided people with a convenient theory that they could use in order to interpret the evidence in the way that they wanted to.

When I look at the world I see evidence for God everywhere. Comparing the theistic way of looking at the world with the atheistic way of looking at the world is just like the effect produced by the Necker Cube. It is a complete shift in perception caused by a radical change of presuppositions. The only difference is that, unlike the Necker Cube, both interpretations cannot both be true. If Dawkins is right, then I am wrong, and vice versa. It is not just a matter of opinion.

This shift in perception between theism and atheism is not dissimilar to the difference between watching a magic trick when you know how it's done, and watching the same trick when you don't know how it's done. You look at things from a completely different point of view. Your eyes will look in different places, recognise significance in different aspects of the performance (for example, a clever use of words that adds to the deception), your sense of wonder may move from the magical effect itself to a wondrous appreciation of the skill involved in a clever sleight that you know has just been performed. It will be almost like you are seeing something totally different, and I think this is the case with Christians and atheists when they look at the world. Although they see the same world, it is as though they are seeing two completely different worlds.

The obvious difference between these two situations though is that if you tell somebody how a magic trick is done, they will almost always accept the explanation and, if they watch the trick again, they will be one of the converted, so to speak. Usually they will not resist believing the explanation in order to continue believing in the magic because their will doesn't care which explanation is the true one. But of course this is not always the case. There are many people who continue to believe in particular fraudulent mediums, even after they have been given ample evidence that proves that particular medium is a fraud. In these cases there is usually an overwhelming reason why they *want* to believe in this person that literally makes them blind to the evidence. Could this be at least part of the reason why so many atheists deliberately ignore the evidence for God?

It is interesting for Christians to note the obvious point that the 'not enough evidence' argument goes completely against what the Bible says. According to the Bible, it is not that we do not have enough evidence for God but that we deliberately suppress the evidence that is all around us.[23] Again, we have a Necker Cube effect. Use your presuppositions to choose your interpretation.

The Trouble with Teapots

Both Richard Dawkins and Derren Brown seem to admire Bertrand Russell's teapot. This is an analogy that Russell drew between God and a proposed teapot that could be, right this very minute, hurtling through our solar system. The reason for the analogy is to show that, because both the teapot and God are both highly improbable, it is up to theists to prove that God exists and not up to atheists to prove he doesn't. Here is how Russell originally put it.

> "If I were to suggest that between the Earth and Mars there is a china teapot revolving about the sun in an elliptical orbit, nobody would be able to disprove my assertion provided I were careful to add that the teapot is too small to be revealed even by our most powerful telescopes. But if I were to go on to say that, since my assertion cannot be disproved, it is intolerable presumption on the part of human reason to doubt it, I should rightly be thought to be talking nonsense. If, however, the existence of such a teapot were affirmed in ancient books, taught as the sacred truth every Sunday, and instilled into the minds of children at school, hesitation to believe in its existence would become a mark of eccentricity and entitle the doubter to the attentions of the psychiatrist in an enlightened age or of the Inquisitor in an earlier time."[24]

Derren Brown in *Tricks of the Mind* mentions it when he says

> "One can be a true believer in anything: psychic ability, Christianity or, as Bertrand Russell classically suggested (with irony), in the fact that there is a teapot orbiting the earth. I could believe any of those things with total conviction. But my conviction doesn't make them true." [25]

We won't quibble about whether this non-existent teapot is not orbiting the earth or not orbiting the sun. I don't suppose it really matters. Either way, the analogy depends on the idea that the orbiting teapot and God's existence are both highly improbable, but I think there are at least three problems with this idea.

The first problem is how would you work out how probable it is that an undetectable teapot is orbiting the earth? Presumably you would need plenty of data about similar planets to the earth and whether they had teapots orbiting them. However, if all of these teapots were undetectable you could not obtain this data. There would be no evidence available. It may be that every other planet actually has such a teapot, making it highly probable that our planet has one too. There would be just no way of knowing. For the analogy with God to work, you would have to state that there is *no evidence whatsoever* for the existence of God.

This is where it gets a little strange. From Richard Dawkins' writing alone, you can see that this is not the case. There must be evidence for God, according to Dawkins. Surely if he admits that before 1859 he would have been a theist, he is admitting that there is at least some evidence (for example, the 'apparent design' that he refers to in *The Blind Watchmaker*) that could be interpreted as evidence in favour of God's existence.[26] It's not that in reality there is no evidence that could be used to support a belief in God; it's just that Dawkins gives this evidence a different interpretation. Therefore the teapot analogy fails.

So why is it that in *The God Delusion* Richard Dawkins says that there is no evidence to favour the 'God Hypothesis', as he calls it?[27]

The only way to make sense of this is to assume that when Dawkins says there is no 'evidence' for God, he is using the word 'evidence' in a slightly unusual way. What he actually means is *there is no evidence that he cannot give an atheistic interpretation to*. So, for example, I might say that the fact that the universe came out of nothing could be given as evidence for God, in as much as the idea of God creating it would be a possible explanation as to how this may have come about. Dawkins is saying that provided he could come up with any other, no matter how fanciful, suggestion as to how the universe may have arrived from out of nowhere without God, then the creation of the universe cannot be considered to be evidence for God.

There are three very interesting things to note here. Firstly, as I have suggested, this is not what most people mean by evidence. To say there is no evidence at all for God, you have to redefine the word 'evidence'. Richard Dawkins has no problem redefining words though as we will see later. We should expect this.

Secondly, it commits a logical fallacy. Dawkins is saying that because something *could* be interpreted in a particular way (i.e. the atheistic way), then that is necessarily the way in which it *should* be interpreted. Now we know this is not true because of examples such as those of the Necker Cube variety. We should not be surprised to find Richard Dawkins committing logical fallacies though, as we shall see later.

Thirdly, the reasoning is circular. To prove materialism by giving a materialistic interpretation to every event, already assumes materialism to be true. We have already seen how science loads the dice by ruling out any supernatural interpretations of events in advance.

I'm sure you will agree that all of this is really quite fascinating. The point to be remembered from all of this though is simply that to buy into the teapot analogy you have to state that there really is no evidence whatsoever that could be used to support a belief in God. This is obviously a ludicrous suggestion to most people, apart from hardcore Dawkins types who are ready to redefine any word that stands in their way. Most people, I think, would argue that the teapot analogy fails to be convincing.

The analogy also fails because this God, whom Richard Dawkins and Derren Brown say can be compared to an undetectable teapot, claimed to have performed many miracles that a whole nation bore witness to and wrote a book about (a piece of evidence, wouldn't you say?). This God also claims to have been born as a human being at a particular time in history. People became followers of him and wrote more books about him (more evidence?). They also died for him (more evidence?) and many continue to do so. Now, even if you don't believe some of these things, the point is that *nobody is claiming any of this* about the teapot. The simple fact that these things are claimed about the Christian God, is enough to show that the teapot analogy is false.

It also fails, I think, for a more interesting reason. However, bear in mind that if you disagree with this reason, it still fails for the previous reasons.

When you try to apply probability to the existence of God there is a big problem. I will try to illustrate it in the following way.

There is quite a well known example sometimes cited to illustrate a particular aspect of probability. I first came across it in Hugh Laurie's novel *The Gun Seller*[28] but I have since discovered it in various other places. It concerns a man who is so afraid of flying that he goes to see a psychiatrist to get help. He is afraid of flying because of his belief that there would be a bomb on board any plane he travelled on. The psychiatrist fails to help him and so sends the man to see a statistician, who tells him that it is very unlikely for there to be a bomb on an aeroplane – in fact the odds were something like half a million to one. The man, however, is still not happy about this so the statistician asks him if he would be happy if the odds were ten million to one. The man says yes that would make him happy, to which the statistician smiles and says that ten million to one just happens to be the odds that there are two unrelated bombs on board any given plane. Puzzled by how this actually helps him, the man asks the statistician to explain what he means. The statistician replies, "It's simple. You take a bomb on board with you."

Probability is a very strange and fascinating thing. At first glance, it may not be obvious what the problem with the logic in that story actually is. You may think you are actually safer on an aeroplane if you really do take a bomb on board with you. It will probably come as no surprise though to find out that you are not. You see, when you work out the probability of anything, what you are always doing is working out *how likely an event is to happen*, and there are always givens. In the above example, it could be stated like this. Given that you yourself do not take a bomb on board with you, the probability of there being a bomb on board the plane is one in half a million. However, given that you do take a bomb on board with you, the probability *for you* of there now being two bombs on the plane is still one in half a million. The probability *for everybody else* of there being two bombs on the plane is one in ten million. Now, I find this very interesting. What we are saying is the probability *of the same event*, namely there being two bombs on this particular plane, is different for different people, because the different people have different givens. This is very important. (By the way, it is probably worth mentioning now that I borrowed the figures of half a million and ten million to one from Hugh Laurie's version of the story. They look very dubious and I have no idea where they came from. However, since the accuracy of these figures makes no difference to the point I am making, I won't quibble with them.)

Another example of this could be a card trick. I might ask you to choose a card at random and then place it back into the deck for you. If it really has been placed randomly into the deck and I have no idea where it is, the probability of me finding it by also randomly picking out a card are one in fifty-two. If I knew that the card was somewhere in the top half of the deck, then the probability of me finding the card would be one in twenty-six. If, however, I managed to fool you into thinking I'd placed your card into the middle of the deck, when really I had kept your card on the top of the deck (perhaps using

Derren Brown's splendid Velvet Turnover move[29] as described in his book *Pure Effect*) I would have a probability of one of finding your card, because I would know exactly where it was. The different givens affect the probability.

So what is wrong with comparing the probability of a teapot orbiting the earth with the probability of God existing? Well, it seems to me that because probability is a way of calculating *how likely it is that an event will happen*, if I wanted to work out the probability of a teapot being in orbit around the earth, what I would really mean is something like, given that this teapot exists, what is the probability that it has at some time been placed into orbit around the earth and is still there?

The problem with working out the probability of God's existence is that the Christian God *is not an event that happens*. He is the ultimate given (by which I mean that within a Christian framework, any statement can be restated by tagging '*Given that God exists...*' on to the start of it). Even within a neutral framework (if such a thing existed, which it doesn't) the Christian God is either there or he isn't. You can't imagine a time when the Christian God didn't exist and then ask what the probability is that he might come into existence. As soon as you try to imagine such a thing, the god you are imagining coming into existence is not the Christian God.

In order to make the teapot analogy work, you have to use a god *that comes into existence*. That is the only way you can speak of working out the probability of God existing. In order to make use of probability in *The God Delusion*, Richard Dawkins has to speak of God as "being evolved" and "arriving late in the universe." He says that "God, in this sense defined, is a delusion."[30] But Christians could have told you that. God here, *in this sense defined*, that *arrives*, is not the Christian God, and Dawkins surely must realise this. It is just that unless he conveniently redefines God as a being *that comes into existence*, the teapot analogy simply doesn't work.

If the Christian God exists at all, then he has always existed. If he does not exist, then he has never existed. Probability is simply not an appropriate tool in this situation, and if the Christian God does exist and he stubbornly refuses to play your little maths games, then that is your problem, not God's. If the Christian God is who he claims to be, then he sets the rules. You cannot simply redefine him so as to provide a convenient excuse for not believing in him. Many people seem to like to think that you can.

The god Richard Dawkins uses here is what we call a straw man. This is a way of misrepresenting an opponent's position. To 'set up a straw man' is to create a position that is easy to refute, then to attribute that position to your opponent. By refuting the straw man, you can give the illusion of having refuted your opponent's actual argument, when in reality you have not even addressed it at all. It's a magic trick, and like most good tricks, Dawkins performs the main sleight right under our very noses.

Let's take a look at more of these kinds of thing and see what they have to do with Richard Dawkins and Derren Brown.

4. Sleight of Mind

The Unreliable Narrator

What I would like to do in this chapter is look at some of the methods used by Derren Brown in his magical performances, and compare them with some of the techniques Richard Dawkins uses in his writing. If my hypothesis is true, and there is a deep link between the two, we should be able to find some examples of this. There are bound to be many other examples that I will not mention but hopefully, the ones I list here will be enough to convince you that the general point I am attempting to make is true; namely that just as Derren Brown uses trickery to perform his magic, Richard Dawkins uses a similar sort of trickery when constructing his arguments. I will begin by considering something called the principle of the unreliable narrator.

An unreliable narrator (a term coined by Wayne C. Booth in his 1961 book *The Rhetoric of Fiction*) is a literary device in which the credibility of the narrator is seriously compromised, sometimes due to a powerful bias, a lack of knowledge, or even a deliberate attempt to deceive the reader or audience. Both Derren Brown and Richard Dawkins are unreliable narrators.

When we watch Derren Brown perform, we should always be aware that he is attempting to deceive us. Much of what he says about what he is actually doing is false. In magic, this is just par for the course. If a performer were completely honest, the tricks wouldn't work. We are all aware of this whenever we watch a magician perform. However, the more honest the magician can convince you that he is being, the more impressive the trick will appear to be.

The unreliable narrator principle has been put to great use over the last decade or so by film-makers to produce some great films (such as *The Sixth Sense, The Usual Suspects, Fallen* and *Memento*, to name but a few) and it was also famously used by

Agatha Christie in one of her most popular detective stories, *The Murder of Roger Ackroyd*.[1]

Richard Dawkins, in *The God Delusion*, is an unreliable narrator because he is not giving a balanced view of religion; he is obviously very strongly biased towards atheism. He also has a lack of knowledge when it comes to religion, which is dangerous as it means he often makes statements and claims about religion that are simply untrue. On top of all that, he will be trying to influence you by the way he uses language. In this chapter we will take a look at some of these techniques.

The Argument by Authority

An argument by authority is a type of argument where an assertion is deemed to be true based on the authority or position of the person asserting it.

When performing mind reading, in order to make the performance convincing, it is vital that the performer projects a certain kind of authority. Watch Derren Brown perform and you will see that he is a master of this, always appearing to be in complete control of the situation. It is this sense of authority that makes his performances so believable.

One of the reasons people may be persuaded to believe the things Richard Dawkins says in *The God Delusion* is precisely because it is Richard Dawkins who is saying them. In magic, this is the idea of context.[2] If an experiment in mindreading is conducted in a science lab, people may take it seriously. If it is conducted by a man on a stage in a sparkly suit and top hat, they may not take it quite so seriously. If I, being a nobody, told you to believe that black and white were really the same thing, you would probably just think I was deluded. If Richard Dawkins told you the same thing, you might be inclined to think about it for a little bit longer. I mean, there must be something in it if Richard Dawkins is saying it. Maybe there is some scientific principle to do with colours that I am not aware of. After all, our senses are complicated things. Who knows what the brain is capable of?

The God Delusion makes good use of this principle right from the outset. On the inside cover it tells us that Richard Dawkins was recently voted one of the world's top three intellectuals by *Prospect* magazine. What would be the point of saying this if it were not meant to add weight to the arguments given in the book? Of course, there is nothing wrong in simply arguing that an assertion made by an expert is *likely* to be true, but remember that Richard Dawkins is *not* an expert in theology at all. In fact, he is not even sure that the subject really exists; a statement he makes several times in *The God Delusion*.[3]

Exploiting Ignorance

Most if not all magic tricks, as I'm sure you realise, rely on the participants being ignorant of the particular methods being used. For example, the ouija board sequence in Derren Brown's *Séance* relied on the participants being ignorant of the ideomotor suggestion principle.[4]

If there is one technique that *The God Delusion* demonstrates brilliantly, it is how to exploit people's ignorance. This is particularly noticable in how Richard Dawkins handles the so-called 'Arguments for God's Existence.' After warming up with a little gentle mockery, he says of Thomas Aquinas's 'proofs' involving an infinite regress that even if we allow ourselves "the dubious luxury" of suggesting that God might be a suitable terminator for an infinite regress, we have no right to attribute to this God all of his other attributes (omnipotence, omniscience, goodness etc.)[5]

This argument relies on the reader being completely ignorant to the whole point of Aquinas's argument. It is not meant to do anything other than call your attention to the fact that if we do not have a being something like God, then we are left with an infinite regress, which is a problem (for other reasons that I won't go into here, as any of these things can be easily looked up in a book such as Norman Geisler's *Baker Encyclopedia of Christian Apologetics*). That is all the argument does. It is simply a pointer that suggests one possible reason why a world with God in it would make more sense than a world without God in it. For God's other attributes, we have different arguments that work in different ways, gradually building up a cumulative case that strongly suggests that a theistic worldview makes more sense of the available evidence than an atheistic worldview. That is all these arguments are meant to do. None of them claim to prove everything there is to be known about God. The only person who seems to believe that is Richard Dawkins, although technically he believes that they *do* prove everything there is to be known about God, since in his opinion they prove nothing and there is nothing to be known. Dawkins continues with a little more mockery (to try to mask his general lack of good arguments, which of course he doesn't believe he really needs to provide), reciting a little limerick that claims to understand God's omnipotence and omniscience so well as to be able to prove their incompatibility in four lines of witty verse, before moving on to a nonsense poem by Edward Lear. On the following page he states that "the argument from design is the only one still in regular use today"; a statement which is completely untrue and again exploits the ignorance of the reader. It may be the only one *he* hears regularly, as he spends most of his time arguing the case for Darwinian evolution. He dismisses the design argument simply by mentioning Darwin's 'clever reasoning' and on he goes to the next one, which happens to be the Ontological Argument. He calls this argument 'infantile'[6], then spends the next three pages not really saying why, until he finally mumbles something about Kant having disproved the argument by questioning whether existence is more perfect than non-existence. He then continues with a few more pages of mockery, before ending with a few comical proofs for the existence of God that he has found on the Internet.

Is this really what Richard Dawkins thinks you have to do to engage with these arguments? Substitute logic for mockery? Only a completely ignorant reader would fail to realise that the only people Dawkins' could possibly convince with any of these contentless 'arguments' would be people as ignorant as he is pretending to be; but then those people, being actually ignorant, would fail to realise this and probably end up thinking that this was quite a good chapter. They could put the book down, still chuckling at the hilarious proofs from the Internet, safe in the knowledge that they were right all along, and Dawkins' book has just confirmed this. Such people would do well to remember Stephen Fry's advice in *The Book of General Ignorance* concerning people 'who think they know what there is to be known' and think that everything can be explained in a particular book that they may happen to endorse. This comment could just as easily be applied to *The God Delusion* as it could to the Bible. It would have been interesting to hear what Dawkins had to say about Alvin Plantinga's formulation of the Ontological Argument, maybe Pascal's Anthropic Argument, or even Peter Berger's 'signals of transcendence'; all of which I find particularly fascinating and persuasive.

The Self-Defeating Argument

In one of his previous books, *A Devil's Chaplain*, Dawkins warns his daughter (and us, the readers) about believing things purely because they have been told to us by a figure of authority. He says in an essay entitled *A Prayer For My Daughter*,

> "...first I must deal with the two other bad reasons for believing in anything; authority and revelation. Authority, as a reason for believing something, means believing it because you are told to believe it by somebody important."[7]

But why should we take any notice of this warning? Why should we believe Richard Dawkins when he has just told us not to believe people because they are somebody important? According to Richard Dawkins' own advice, we shouldn't believe him. This is what is known as a self-defeating argument.

Some statements, as well as arguments, are self defeating. Take, for example, the sentence *'This sentence is not true'*. Is this sentence true? If it is true, then it is false. However, if it is false, then it is true. This paradox is caused by the fact that the sentence is self-referencing (something that caused Bertrand Russell a whole lot of trouble in 1931 at the hands of logician Kurt Gödel, but that's another story). Another similar example of this sort of paradox is the sentence *'I am a liar'*. If somebody says that, are they telling the truth? If we take it to mean that everything they say is a lie, then if they are lying, then they are not. If they are not lying, then they are.

As a magician, Derren Brown is permanently trapped inside the 'I am a liar' paradox. He makes various claims of honesty in several places but we always know that he is a professional liar. How do we know that his claims of honesty aren't just more lies?

In *Tricks of the Mind*, he mentions the problem of honesty with reference to magical performances. He says that the magician basically says to his audience, "I'm going to act as if this were all very real; but you know, and I know that you know that I know, that it's really a game."[8] He goes on to say that, in *Tricks of the Mind*, although he cannot be "impossibly open", he promises to be "entirely honest."[9]

Do you believe him? I want to. I really do want to.

The Circular Argument

Also sometimes referred to as 'begging the question', a circular argument is one in which at least one of the premises presupposes the conclusion in some way, resulting in there being no reason to believe the conclusion.

This is a big problem for somebody like Richard Dawkins. Our belief, or disbelief, in God is so foundational to the way we think about everything that it cannot help but make its presence felt behind almost every statement we make, particularly in a discussion that is, after all, about God. The same can be said for the idea of Darwinian evolution. So many of Richard Dawkins' arguments presuppose the truth of evolution (as you would expect, since his worldview is so saturated by it) that, if you are not entirely convinced that the 'fact' of evolution really is a fact, many of his arguments simply fall flat. (To give a couple of quick examples to illustrate my point; his idea of God being necessarily complex presupposes evolution – in fact more than that, it presupposes that God himself evolved – and his saying that we are all very improbable beings presupposes atheism, since our improbability stems from our complexity, and our complexity only implies improbability if there is no God to design us.)

From a Christian point of view, the Bible give us this advice in Proverbs 26:4

> "Do not answer a fool according to his folly
>   or you will be like him yourself
>
> Answer a fool according to his folly
>   or he will be wise in his own eyes."

In the case of *The God Delusion*, the folly is, of course, atheism. 'Do not answer a fool according to his folly' means that sometimes we should not adopt the same presuppositions as our opponent. We should simply state our case, boldly asserting what we believe, in the hope that people will see the truth in what we are saying. Anything we say in this manner will, of course, be in a sense circular because I will be trying to prove the existence of God, whilst presupposing his existence and letting this presupposition colour everything I say. The alternative is to 'answer a fool according to his folly', meaning that sometimes it is good to assume your opponent's point of view is true, and then try to show that it leads to something obviously unacceptable or just plain silly. If this is the case, then your opponent's point of view must be false. This is what I attempted to do with materialism in my 'Trigger's broom' example. This kind of argument is called 'reductio ad absurdum' or 'proof by contradiction'. Most of the 'Arguments for God's Existence' can be stated in this form (for example, we could give the Moral Argument by assuming that God does not exist, and attempting to show that this leads to there being no such thing as real evil. If you do not accept that there is no such thing as real evil, then you must conclude that the starting point was false and that God actually does exist). A typical argument of this type used against God could be what is typically referred to as the Problem of Evil. Assume God exists and try to persuade people that if this were the case, there would not be so much evil in the world. If you agree that there is an unacceptable amount of evil in the world, then you must conclude that God does not exist. Richard Dawkins does not use many arguments of this type in *The God Delusion*, probably because, if he did, he would be treating theology as if it were a real subject, which of course he doesn't believe it is. Most of his arguments are of the first kind and, as a result, are often viciously circular. It is sometimes possible to mask the circularity of an argument somewhat by making the circles bigger. For example, you could say something like, if atheism is true, then there is no other way, apart from Darwinian evolution, that we could have all got here. Then you could argue that since we all got here by Darwinian evolution, we should all reject the idea of God. I think it's fair to say that there is evidence for this particular kind argument in the writings of Richard Dawkins.

The Argument by Confusion

Starting on page 216 of *Tricks of the Mind*, Derren Brown tells a rather amusing anecdote about something that happened to him one night in Llandudno. On his way home from a magic convention, he was threatened by a "very aggressive Welsh drunk" whom Derren made the fatal mistake of looking at.

Rather than attempting to fight the man, he managed to escape being beaten up and stabbed by simply confusing him to such an extent that he "sat down on the kerb, distraught and broken." It's a great story. The idea is that by confusing somebody, you can make them more open to accepting your point of view; in Derren's case, the point of view that it is nice not to be stabbed to death. Here is how describes this effect.

> "The state of bewilderment he was in would also have rendered him highly suggestible. The use of disorienting techniques to amplify a person's responsiveness to suggestion is a classic ploy of talented persuaders. A politician knows that if he fires a set of confusing statistics at listeners, followed by a 'summing up', they are more likely to believe that concluding statement."[10]

This is the technique that Derren has claimed to be using to send the people to sleep when they answer the telephone[11] (although I would imagine that many people think this is likely to be a pseudo-explanation; we'll come to those later).

Now, what does this have to do with Richard Dawkins? Turn, if you have it, to page 56 of *The God Delusion* and read the passage (I won't quote it in full here as it is quite long) that starts with "It is a tedious cliché" and ends with "imply that religion can." It starts about two thirds of the way down the page and it works better if you read it quickly.

His 'summing up' at the end is that if science cannot answer a question, this does not imply that religion can. Do you believe him? You should, because what else could possibly be the point of all that odd stuff that comes before it? He asks what on earth is a why question? Well, surely it's a question that starts with the word 'why', isn't it, or am I missing something deeper here? Surely Dawkins is not suggesting that any question beginning with the word 'why' is meaningless? He says that not every English sentence beginning with the word 'why' is a legitimate question. Well, no. That is true. Neither is every sentence beginning with the word 'how'. I can make up a meaningless sentence beginning with any word I like. What has this got to do with whether religion can answer questions that science can't?

Although I find it hard to believe, and I admit that I might be mistaken because it seems so strange, I think that the only explanation is that Richard Dawkins is doing what Derren Brown did. We are the aggressive Welsh drunks here, and very soon we're going to be sitting down on a kerb, distraught and broken, saying, "Of course God doesn't exist. How stupid of me for not seeing it before. My questions about God were all meaningless."

Seriously though, this really is a very odd paragraph. When I think of the amount of time I am spending now, trying to make sure that I am constructing clear, logical arguments, there just doesn't seem to be any other explanation for what he is doing.

It's worth mentioning, just as an aside, that Dawkins is right when he says that just because science cannot answer a question, it does not imply that religion can. It is also true, however, that because science cannot answer a question, it does not imply that religion can't. What science can or can't do does not imply anything about what religion can or can't do at all.

The Kellogg's Cornflakes Suggestion

In one of his previous books, *Absolute Magic*, Derren Brown has said that if you want to get somebody to believe something, the best way to go about it is not just to tell them outright. He claims that the best way to get somebody to believe something is to offer them a sentence that implies what you are really trying to say, but in a seemingly unintentional way.[12] This, Derren Brown says, is an application of 'suggestion'.

On page 162 of *Tricks of the Mind*, we find Derren Brown giving us advice on how to hypnotise people. Kellogg's, he says, used to advertise Cornflakes with the slogan 'Have you forgotten how good they taste?' The reason that they chose this slogan was because they wanted you to believe that Cornflakes tasted good and this question gets the point across in a rather clever way. How it works is that the question that is asked presupposes what the speaker actually wants to communicate, and questions something peripheral to the real message. In other words, while thinking about whether you have forgotten how good they taste, you forget to question whether they actually do taste good at all.

So, he says, an example of something you might say to somebody while hypnotising them, is "You can wonder how deeply you are going into a trance," because this question presupposes that they actually *are* going into a trance.

Now what does this have to do with Richard Dawkins? Do you remember the strange answer he gave to the question of whether science was able to offer consolation in the same way that religion does? This was his response.

> "The fact that religion may console you doesn't of course make it true. It's a moot point whether one wishes to be consoled by a falsehood."[13]

If you recall, Alister McGrath pointed out that this was bad logic because it does not follow that something is false, simply because it has not been proven.

Surely this is a classic example of what we will from now on call the "Kellogg's Cornflakes Suggestion". What Richard Dawkins says is, "It's a moot point whether one wishes to be consoled by a falsehood." This is just what Derren Brown has been talking about. Dawkins' response presupposes that religion is 'a falsehood'. He masks this presupposition, that we will be subconsciously influenced to accept, by asking a peripheral question about whether or not we want to be consoled by a falsehood. It's brilliant.

He does a similar, but not quite the same, thing on page 73 of *The God Delusion* when he says, before giving his reasons for disbelieving in the existence of God, that it is his responsibility to "dispose of the positive arguments for belief." This bold claim presupposes that he is actually able to 'dispose of the positive arguments for belief.' In this case though, rather than the idea he wants us to accept being masked by a peripheral question, it is masked by the tremendous confidence and almost casual way in which the claim is made. He completely downplays the magnitude of what it is he is subconsciously telling us he is able to do.

Derren Brown uses this technique too, making bold claims in a casual way. It's standard practice. For example, as a preamble to a book test he performed in one of his live shows, he almost casually said that before each show he memorises the whole telephone directory for the city in which the show is taking place. He then proceeds to have people shout out names, to which he replies with their telephone number. What is surprising (although maybe it shouldn't be) is that many people leave the show actually wondering whether he really did memorise the whole telephone directory. It really is an incredibly useful technique.

The False Analogy
In an analogy, it is claimed that because two concepts or objects are similar to each other in one respect, they must also be similar in another respect.

Before we even get into the first chapter of *The God Delusion*, Richard Dawkins dedicates the book to Douglas Adams, the writer of the immensely popular novel *The Hitchhiker's Guide to the Galaxy*. Underneath Adams' name appears this quotation.

"Isn't it enough to see that a garden is beautiful without having to believe that there are fairies at the bottom of it too?"

In *The God Delusion*, Richard Dawkins in several places makes an analogy between God and fairies. The way in which they are similar, according to Dawkins, is that although strictly you can't disprove the existence of either one of them, neither is there any evidence for the existence of either one of them. On page 52, he speaks of someone who "is an a-theist to exactly the same large extent that he is an a-fairyist." They are both childish beliefs that ought to be abandoned when we grow up.

However, as Alister McGrath has pointed out, the analogy here is a false one. He says in his book, *Dawkins' God*

"As I noticed while researching *The Twilight of Atheism*, a large number of people come to believe in God in later life – when they are "grown up." I have yet to meet anyone who came to believe in Santa Claus or the Tooth Fairy late in life."[14]

In *Tricks of the Mind*, Derren Brown says that a false analogy works particularly well if it provides a good mental picture of a situation.[15] Hopefully, we will see some examples of this later.

The Straw Man
There is a popular magic trick, made famous by David Blaine but also mentioned in Derren Brown's excellent book *Pure Effect*[16] called *Cigarette through Pound Coin* (translated from the original American *Cigarette-thru-Quarter*). In case you don't know what happens in this trick (although the title pretty much sums it up), the magician asks a volunteer to lend him a pound coin. He tells the people watching that every coin has a soft spot somewhere in it and if you search hard enough you can... at this point the audience are stunned to see the magician push a cigarette through the middle of the coin. The

method, as I will state here as obviously there is no other way it could possibly be done, is that the magician basically switches the spectator's coin for a gimmicked one with a hole in the middle of it and that, in many but not quite all ways, is that. The magic is created by a clever coin switch.

The straw man fallacy is very much like the *Cigarette through Pound Coin* trick. The only difference is that instead of switching a real coin for a fake coin in order to punch a big hole in it, Richard Dawkins switches the real God for a fake god, real religion for his own version of religion, and real faith for his own caricature of faith, in order to punch big holes in them.

Remember that a straw man argument is a way of misrepresenting an opponent's position. To 'set up a straw man' is to create a position that is easy to refute, then to attribute that position to your opponent. By refuting the straw man, you can give the illusion of having refuted your opponent's actual argument, when in reality you have not even addressed it at all.

Dawkins definition of faith is very interesting. In his 1976 book, *The Selfish Gene*, he defined faith to be "blind trust, in the absence of evidence, even in the teeth of evidence."[17] He goes further by saying

> "But what, after all, is faith? It is a state of mind that leads people to believe something – it doesn't matter what – in the total absence of supporting evidence. If there were good supporting evidence, then faith would be superfluous, for the evidence would compel us to believe it anyway."[18]

In his book, *Dawkins' God*, Alister McGrath comments that he has never met anyone else who defines faith in this way.[19] It is Dawkins' own definition, constructed with his own agenda in mind. McGrath says

"This arbitrary and idiosyncratic definition simply does not stand up to serious investigation. In fact, it is itself an excellent example of a belief tenaciously held and defended 'in the absence of evidence, even in the teeth of evidence.'"[20]

Surely though, it is also worth noticing that what we have here from Dawkins is a false dichotomy (something to which we will return shortly). He seems to be saying that there are only two types of beliefs; those for which there is no evidence at all and those for which the evidence is compelling. Surely most, if not all of, our beliefs fall somewhere in between those two extremes. Only a reader who is not thinking at all could accept a statement like this.

Now let's consider the word 'religion'. This is a word that is often defined in very different ways. I will look at just two definitions from two different sources. *Merriam-Webster's Online Dictionary* defines religion as "a cause, principle, or system of beliefs held to with ardour and faith." One obvious approach when dealing with atheism is to make the point that atheism can itself be considered a religion. If religion is to be defined in the way *Merriam-Webster's Online Dictionary* defines it, then I don't really see how you can say anything against that view. Materialistic atheism has a creed; namely Carl Sagan's "The cosmos is all that is, or ever was, or ever will be."[21] It certainly has faith, in the usual sense of the word. To reject everything supernatural is clearly an act of faith, since it is not something that could ever be proved scientifically – particularly when science is naturally biased to reject anything supernatural, however strong the evidence might be. The idea that life could arise from non-life without the help of God is also something that must be believed as an act of faith. So how does Richard Dawkins say in *The God Delusion* that atheists do not have faith?[22] Of course, we know exactly how he does it. He redefines the word 'faith'. The same goes for the idea of atheism being a religion. Dawkins does not like this idea, because he is writing a book about how awful religion is. His book needs to be broad enough in scope to encompass every belief system that he wants to attack, but no so broad that it includes his own belief system. The way he gets around the problem is by using a different definition of religion, better suited to his purpose. The *Concise Oxford Dictionary* defines religion as "Human recognition of superhuman controlling power and especially of a personal God entitled to obedience." By this definition, atheism is not a religion, but then neither is Buddhism. Dawkins knows this.[23] But do we really want to be using a definition of religion that excludes Buddhism? As problematic as this sounds, there is strictly nothing wrong with choosing a definition of a word that suits your particular argument, as long as you define it up front before you begin to make your argument. Problems can occur though if what you mean by a particular word is not what your reader would generally mean by it. In order to understand you correctly, the reader must continually keep in mind *your* definition of the word and not theirs. This, obviously, provides a great opportunity for confusing the reader by legitimate means.

For a book like *The God Delusion*, it is unfortunate that one of the words Dawkins may very likely be defining rather differently to many of the readers is the word 'God' itself. This is very confusing. However, the book does not automatically become totally meaningless to the reader as long as there is some overlap between the two definitions. If we compare Dawkins' definition of God with the Christian definition of God, we find that they are both supernatural beings, in the sense of being immaterial. There we have some common ground. However, we have already seen that Dawkins' god is a god that comes into existence, whereas the Christian God has always existed. Unfortunately, this difference in definition makes, for Christians, some of the arguments in *The God Delusion* completely irrelevant.

Caricatures and stereotypes (other straw men) abound in Dawkins' book. The only thing that religious people cling to, in a desperate attempt to give some credibility to their blind faith, is the argument from design. Religious people generally are either insane or wicked and when, for example, he decides to make a television programme to back up this point of view, he is very careful about how he selects his biased sample of people to interview. It would be equivalent to me making a programme called *Science: The Root of All Evil?* and starting off by profiling Josef Mengele, the Nazi 'Angel of Death', followed by The Nutty Professor.

The Straw Straw Man

One step further than the Straw Man is what we may as well call the Straw Straw Man. This is where a straw man is deliberately set up as a cover for another straw man. Usually when you knock down a straw man you replace it with a true definition. In the Straw Straw Man, rather than being accused of using a straw man argument, you anticipate this by setting up a straw man that you never intend to use, knocking it down yourself and replacing it with another straw man that you will use, hoping that your reader will think you are being fair and that your new straw man is the real thing.

Dawkins does this with God in *The God Delusion*, when he says that he wants to prevent himself from being accused of using a straw man god in the sky with a long beard. Instead he says he is attacking all gods, by which he means anything and everything supernatural.[24] This sentence, in the process of trying to be general, ends up not defining God at all. In fact, if you remember, he has already given his definition of the god he is attacking. This is the god who 'evolved' and 'arrived' in the universe.[25] Here Dawkins is saying that this is the definition of God he will be using in later chapters and, as we've already seen, God, *in this sense defined*, is nothing but another straw man.

Andy Nyman, Derren Brown's co-writer suggests a good example of the Straw Straw Man in a trick on his DVD, *The Andy Nyman Lecture*.[26] In this trick he asks a member of the audience to think of a film and name it. What he sometimes does in this trick (and again I am being deliberately careful not to give away any real details) is knock down a straw man method in which he could have cheated in order to imply that he has not cheated at all. Of course, it goes without saying that he has cheated and his dismissal of one method is only a clever means of concealing another.

Affirming the Consequent

On page 5 of *The God Delusion*, Richard Dawkins quotes Robert Pirsig's book, *Zen and the Art of Motorcycle Maintenance*, which says

> "When one person suffers from a delusion, it is called insanity. When many people suffer from a delusion it is called Religion."[27]

Dawkins says that he is in agreement with Pirsig, with regard to religion being a "symptom of a psychiatric disorder". What is interesting to notice here is that, contrary to what he is implying, Dawkins and Pirsig are *strictly* saying *opposite* things. Pirsig is saying 'When many people suffer from a delusion, it is called Religion' which is, I suppose, possibly a true statement, since this is at least true of all false religions (and some religions have to be false because different religions contradict each other). What Dawkins is saying is *therefore all religions are a symptom of a psychiatric disorder*; in other words all religions are delusions. Pirsig says A implies B, and Dawkins says therefore B implies A. Pirsig's statement leaves us with the possibility (I admit, maybe not intentionally) that at least one religion is not a delusion. Dawkins' statement does not. This is an example of a logical fallacy called 'affirming the consequent'.

Affirming the consequent means assuming the converse of a statement to be true when it may not be. In other words because A implies B, it is assumed that B implies A. A simple example of this could be 'If a shape is a square, then it has four sides'. That statement is true. The converse statement 'If a shape has four sides, then it is a square' is, of course, false.

It could be argued that magicians do this all the time in order to make themselves believable. For example, if Derren Brown were really able to read your mind, he could tell you exactly what word you were thinking of right now (A implies B). Therefore, if he can tell you exactly what word you are thinking of right now, he must be able to read your mind (B implies A). At least, that is how it is meant to appear. He convinces you that he can read minds by appearing to do the things that a real mind reader would be able to do; in fact, he very strongly stresses this point in his writings, that a spectator must feel that the mind-reader is acting in the way a real mind-reader would act.

Affirming the consequent can also be present in a more subtle way, and it can work a little like one of Derren Brown's mothods of suggestion. Richard Dawkins hints at this when, in *A Devil's Chaplain*, he says that he no longer debates creationists because it gives them an appearance of respectability and makes it look, to ignorant spectators, that there is even something worth debating.[28]

He also makes the same point in *The God Delusion*. The fact that there is a debate at the moment between evolutionists and creationists is undeniable. Concerned though, with the amount of media attention creationists are getting, Dawkins now refuses to debate them. The logic seems to go something like this. If there really were nothing worth debating, I would not have to bother debating creationists. Therefore, if I refuse to debate them, it will make people think that there is nothing worth debating. It's a bit like a magic trick. I create the effect that there is nothing worth debating by acting in the way that I would act if there really were nothing worth debating. Isn't that great? Obviously, if there were nothing to debate and everything was as simple and clear cut as Dawkins makes out, then he could easily go and debate creationists and effortlessly demolish any arguments that they might present, but he simply isn't able to do this.

Reductionism and Caricatures

Another method of misleading people is to give an explanation of a situation that I will call reductionist. What I mean by this is that it explains a given situation very well, as long as you ignore certain aspects of it. If you can convince people that the parts you are ignoring don't exist, or simply take advantage of the fact that they may forget they exist, then you can convince them that your explanation is a good one.

All magic uses this principle, as each trick depends on the spectator being unaware of a certain aspect of what is going on; namely the method behind the trick. If I were to make a playing card leave the deck and float around my body, the spectator may conclude that the best, if not the only, explanation for this is that I have magical powers. This explanation would probably be arrived at because the spectator was ignorant of something that was actually present in the situation; for example, a piece of invisible thread attached to my body.

Derren Brown gives an excellent reductionist explanation when he tells us how he beat the grand masters at chess in his *Trick of the Mind* television series. He simply paired the players off, and used the moves of each player in the pair against the other player in the pair, so the pairs of chess players were actually playing each other, only using Derren to make their moves for them. This was a great explanation; right up to the point where he showed us that there were an odd number of chess players, meaning that he still had to play, and beat, one of the chess grand masters himself.

This is often what happens when somebody gives a reductionist explanation. It will work up to a point but there will invariably be awkward facts that do not seem to fit; a bit like when you take something apart and put it back together only to find a few pieces left over. In my opinion, the materialistic (non-supernatural) view of the world is reductionist. By stripping away the spiritual dimension (in this case by denying its existence) it makes it hard to explain various things such as consciousness, morality, desire, and spiritual experiences. Most of these have (in one worldview or another) been written off as delusions, but this does not satisfy everybody. Another problem like this is the one I described using Trigger's broom as an illustration. Most 'Arguments for God's Existence' attempt to use these kind of ideas to show people how a theistic worldview might better explain all the evidence than a materialistic, atheistic worldview.

Bertrand Russell's Teapot is an example of a reductionist analogy. The analogy only works if you ignore Christianity's history. If the belief that there is a teapot orbiting the earth was backed up by the maker of the teapot claiming to have come to earth to tell us about it, followed by a book being written all about it by people who were prepared to die because they were convinced that they had good evidence that the teapot is really there, followed by two thousand years filled with people who claimed to have had encounters with the creator of the teapot, I think we should be inclined to take the claim at least a little more seriously. We may still decide not to believe in it, but surely it would be worth investigating.

G. K. Chesterton had something interesting to say about delusions in chapter two of his book, *Orthodoxy*.[29] The chapter is called 'The Maniac' and in it Chesterton argues that people who are deluded often have a reductionist view of the world. I will not go into the details of the argument, but I recommend that anybody interested in following this line of reasoning should read what Chesterton has to say. When Robert Pirsig said that 'when many people suffer from a delusion it is called Religion', this could, of course, apply to either Christianity or atheism. According to Chesterton, what we should be asking, if we want to decide which group is deluded, is which view of the world appears to be the most reductionist? To me it seems that atheism is more reductionist. If I asked an atheist how the universe came into existence, he would not really have an answer. Of course, he may try to cover up this fact by mumbling something about vacuum fluctuations and virtual particles but what it would come down to is that he has no idea how the universe came into existence out of nothing. A Christian could at least say that God made it. This, to me, is a very good explanation. To Richard Dawkins, it would be no explanation at all because, remember, he has already presupposed God out of existence.

A caricature can simply be thought of as a reductionist, although in some ways exaggerated, description of something. In *The God Delusion*, Dawkins gives us a quotation that demonstrates how powerfully deceptive a caricature can be. It is at the beginning of a chapter called *'What's wrong with religion? Why be so hostile?'* and the quotation, from George Carlin, says the following.

> "Religion has actually convinced people that there's an invisible man – living in the sky – who watches everything you do, every minute of every day. And the invisible man has a special list of ten things he does not want you to do. And if you do any of these ten things, he has a special place, full of fire and smoke and burning and torture and anguish, where he will send you to live and suffer and burn and choke and scream and cry forever and ever 'til the end of time... But He loves you!"[30]

Now, what can you say about that? Well, to say nothing of the particular style of rhetoric being used by Carlin here, it has to be said that the description is hideously reductionist in nature. Even if you agreed that what he says is mostly true, what he is describing is not the message of Christianity. Christianity does teach that God can see all that we do, and that there are certain things we should not do, and that people who persist in their rebellion against God will ultimately be punished. However, it also teaches that God does not want this to happen. He wants us to follow his rules because he gave them for our benefit. Although his justice demands that evil be punished, he gives us all the option of having our own punishment paid in full for us by none other than God himself in the person of Jesus. That is why we can say he loves us; not because of the fact that he will send us to hell. Hell is a consequence of God's justice, not his love, but of course God's justice is not mentioned here. If we want to avoid being sent to hell, all the Bible says we have to do is trust in Jesus Christ. However, by describing only the 'negative' (for want of a better word) part of Christianity in a very vivid way and then throwing in a casual 'God loves you', Carlin is able to make the whole situation sound ridiculous quite easily, but it's just a cheap trick.

The Appeal to Emotion

An appeal to emotion attempts to win an argument by manipulating someone's emotions, rather than by using a valid logical argument. There is a great example of this in the preface to *The God Delusion*. On the very first page, Richard Dawkins describes an advertisement Channel Four put in the newspaper to promote his two-part television series *Root of All Evil?* This advertisement was a picture of the Manhattan skyline, before 9/11, with the caption 'Imagine a world without religion'.

This is a classic example of an appeal to emotion. Richard Dawkins is obviously trying to say that without religion, 9/11 would never have happened. There is obviously some truth here, as the hijackers were all religious, but is the act of flying a plane into a skyscraper something that religious people generally do? The 9/11 hijackers are not typical of religious people at all. They are not even typical of Muslims. The caption on the picture might just as well have said 'Imagine a world without aeroplanes'. As you can probably appreciate, the appeal to emotion works best when combined with a half truth. It is manipulative, it is a trick, and it proves nothing.

Derren Brown uses this same principle in a more positive way in his book *Tricks of the Mind*. In the section entitled 'Playing with Pictures' he describes a way of motivating yourself to perform a task by making the task look and feel like one that you would naturally feel motivated towards.[31]

Here he is teaching the reader how to transfer a positive emotion, felt for a particular activity, artificially onto another activity in order to feel equally positive about that one. It's a useful idea. Richard Dawkins, however, uses it the other way around. He wants you to transfer the horror you feel about 9/11 to the idea of religion in general. It's another trick.

The Slippery Slope and Association Fallacies

The slippery slope is an argument that one event or trend will initiate a chain of events leading to an undesirable conclusion. It can be either valid or invalid.

An association fallacy is a type of logical fallacy which says that the qualities of one thing are inherently qualities of another, merely by association. Typical types of association fallacy are 'guilt by association' and 'honour by association'.

Richard Dawkins begins the first episode of *Root of All Evil?* by speaking to a group of Roman Catholics on a pilgrimage to Lourdes. As they march through the darkness, holding candles he says

> "It looks lovely doesn't it? Gentle and inoffensive; but isn't this the beginning of that slippery slope that leads to young men with rucksack bombs on the tube?"[32]

This an example of the Slippery Slope Fallacy. Think about what he says. First of all, it's cast as a rhetorical question. Dawkins' implies that the answer is yes, and expects you to automatically accept that without him saying it explicitly. If he had said, "This is the beginning of that slippery slope that leads to young men with rucksack bombs on the tube," you would be more likely to spot the fact that what he is saying is simply untrue. How many Roman Catholic suicide bombers have you read about lately? It seems that, as far as Dawkins is concerned, all religious people are guilty by association.

The Cop Out or "Just too easy" Fallacy

In *The God Delusion*, Richard Dawkins quotes a theologian named Richard Swinburne who gives a theistic definition of God. Here is part of what Swinburne says.

> "What theists claim about God is that he does have a power to create, conserve, or annihilate anything, big or small. God is not limited by the laws of nature; he makes them and he can change or suspend them – if he chooses."[33]

Then Dawkins says, "Just too easy, isn't it!"

The reasoning here is that the explanation is "just too easy", therefore it is probably false. The explanation is considered to be a 'cop out', by which is meant a cowardly or feeble evasion of the truth. In reality though, whether an explanation is simple or complex bears no relation to whether it is true or not. To suggest that it does is just a trick.

Dawkins feels that the theistic explanation of the how the universe works is a cop out. In his opinion, it is an explanation that fails to explain anything and should therefore be ruled out. The problem with this point of view however, is that if the explanation that has been ruled out is actually the true explanation, it leaves science in a bit of a mess because it will never be able to discover the truth if the truth has been ruled out in advance.

It is very similar to when a detective in a movie, presented with a crime that appears to be an open and shut case says, "I don't like it. It's just too easy." (Maybe instead of 'the cop out fallacy' it should be called 'the cop show fallacy'?) What this usually means is that the film makers realise that they have another hour to fill, and open and shut cases generally do not make good detective fiction. What the detective is really saying is that he has a hunch, or a 'gut feeling' that this is too easy. It *feels* too convenient. This is, I'm sure, what Richard Dawkins is saying here. Elsewhere, however, Dawkins praises Carl Sagan for saying that he does not 'think with his gut'.[34] This is a clear case of inconsistency on Dawkins' part. You really can't have it both ways.

In one of his Sherlock Holmes stories, Sir Arthur Conan Doyle describes the disappointment experienced by one of Holmes's clients when the detective explains how he performed one of his characteristically impressive 'deductions'. According to Conan Doyle, it was a case of "omne ignotum pro magnifico", which very roughly translates as "everything unknown is taken for magnificent."[35] In other words, once you know how it's done, it doesn't seem half as impressive as it did before. One of the basic rules of magic is that you never tell somebody how a trick is done. One reason for this is that when you do tell somebody how a trick works, they are often very disappointed by the method. What seemed to be something quite magnificent is usually revealed to be fairly banal. Is it possible that Richard Dawkins is simply disappointed by the Christian explanation of things?

After all, some of the most profound truths we know about the universe can be expressed very simply. Take, for example, Einstein's equation $E = mc^2$. Can you imagine Dawkins going up to Einstein and saying in disbelief, "I don't know, Albert. Don't you think it's just too easy?"

Circular Word Definitions
Richard Dawkins claims to be trying in *The God Delusion* to persuade Christians, and other religious people in general, to become atheists. One subtle trick that he uses is what I will refer to as the circular word definition. This is where he uses a word in a way that only really makes sense if you already presuppose atheism to be true. A simple example of this

comes early in the book, where Dawkins is talking about an Anglican priest who worked as a chaplain at his school. He refers to this priest as a decent liberal clergyman who did not force religion down his throat.[36]

The word in question here is 'decent'. Dawkins seems to be suggesting that what is decent about this clergyman is his liberalism. For the priest to be decent means that he does not take Christianity seriously enough to be concerned about the soul of the young Richard Dawkins; therefore, a negative attitude towards biblical Christianity is here presented as a positive thing, simply by appearing to call somebody 'decent'. It's clever.

Ambiguity and Equivocation

By ambiguity, I mean when someone uses a word or phrase that can have more than one meaning without making it clear which meaning is intended.

A similar concept, equivocation, is when someone uses the same word more than once in an argument and uses it to mean different things, while implying that the word always has the same meaning.

When Derren Brown performed the trick on the tube train, making people forget which stop they were getting off at, he claimed to be using a kind of ambiguity or equivocation in order to add to the confusion he was creating in the minds of the people he approached. He approached one man saying that they were making a documentary. Derren then said to the man, "It's a documentary about how easily trains of thought can become confused," obviously using the word 'train' to refer to a train of thought, while at the same time making him think of the tube 'train' that he was travelling on and rendering the man confused. Whether there was, in reality, more going on here, it is certainly true that when people use the same word to mean two different things it can, sometimes intentionally, be very confusing.

Ambiguous statements often are an integral part of the method behind a successful magic trick. Max Maven, a friend of Derren Brown, has some great examples of this technique on his *Videomind* DVDs, which are well worth getting if you are interested in exploring this sort of thing.

You do not have to look very far to find an example of equivocation in the writings of Richard Dawkins. On the very first page of the Preface to *The Blind Watchmaker* he says this about his computer.

> "The computer was consciously designed and deliberately manufactured."[37]

He then says about the human brain

> "The complexity of living organisms is matched by the elegant efficiency of their apparent design. If anyone doesn't agree that this amount of design cries out for an explanation, I give up."[38]

In the first instance, 'design' with respect to the computer means a process of conceptualisation carried out by a human being. Dawkins then begins a transition between his two meanings by referring to 'apparent design.' It is worth noticing here that the mere apparentness of the 'apparent design' is not apparent from its appearance. 'Apparent design' is apparently, by definition, 'design'. It is only merely apparent, if you already have some reason for presupposing that what you are looking at was not designed – for example, an ideological commitment to materialism. The third time he uses the word 'design' he is not referring to a process of conceptualisation carried out by a human being at all. He is referring to something else, which will turn out to be the result of blind natural selection. However, he would like us to keep thinking of *what we mean by design*, because the design we see around us does indeed cry out for an explanation and so Dawkins' statement appears to make good sense. The explanation of this design that Dawkins gives, however, is one that tells us that what we are seeing is not design. So actually, he does not give us an explanation for design at all – even though he says it is crying out for one. This process of simply doing away with something that you have no explanation for, then pretending that you have explained it, I believe lies at the very heart of *The God Delusion*.

Magic Circularity

So we come round again to Derren Brown's Magic Circularity. Remember the quote from *Tricks of the Mind* about people who believe in the paranormal ignoring evidence that goes against their beliefs and focussing on the evidence that supports their beliefs?[39]

Believe it or not, this doesn't only apply to people who believe in the paranormal. It applies to (you guessed it) Richard Dawkins. This sleight could be called 'only giving one side of the argument and then pretending that what you have said is all that there is to say on the matter' but I prefer to call it 'magic circularity'.

For a book that is almost 400 pages long, *The God Delusion* really does have nothing positive to say about religion at all. It also has nothing negative to say about atheism. On page 1, Dawkins almost immediately starts talking about religion and 'the evils that are done in its name.' When it comes to atheism, however, it is realistic, brave and splendid, and atheists should be happy, balanced and moral. By the time we get to page 3 we find him saying that atheists should be proud of their beliefs as it shows that they have a healthy mind.

In fact, just as Derren Brown says, all the evidence that does not support atheism is ignored. Ravi Zacharias points out in his book *The Real Face of Atheism*

> "In his book *Modern Times*, the historian Paul Johnson referred to Hitler, Stalin and Mussolini as the three devils of the twentieth century."[40]

Who would disagree with this? What is more, all three of them were atheists. In his book, *Dawkins' God*, Alister McGrath says

> "Communism was a 'tragedy of planetary dimensions' with a grand total of victims variously estimated by contributors to the volume [*The Black Book of Communism*] at between 85 million and 100 million."[41]

We will look later at how Richard Dawkins deals with this kind of thing. McGrath concludes by saying

> "One of the greatest ironies of the twentieth century is that many of the most deplorable acts of murder, intolerance, and repression were carried out by those who thought that religion was murderous, intolerant and repressive – and thus sought to remove it from face of the planet as a humanitarian act. Even his most uncritical readers should be left wondering why Dawkins has curiously failed to mention, let alone engage with, the blood-spattered trail of atheism in the twentieth century – one of the reasons, incidentally, that I eventually concluded that I could no longer be an atheist."[42]

Never forget that Richard Dawkins is an unreliable narrator. He is, just like Derren Brown, not going to tell you the whole story.

The Semi-attached Figure

In his classic book *How to Lie with Statistics*, Darrell Huff gave this very funny (at least to statisticians) definition of what he called the semi-attached figure.

> "If you can't prove what you want to prove, demonstrate something else and pretend that they are

the same thing. In the daze that follows the collision of statistics with the human mind, hardly anybody will notice the difference. The semi-attached figure is a device guaranteed to stand you in good stead. It always has."[43]

In *The God Delusion*, Dawkins does something very much like this. On page 50 he talks about placing human judgements about the existence of God along a range of probabilities. To do this, he divides people up into ten categories. Here are a couple of them.

For category one, the strong theist, there is a 100 per cent probability of God. He puts C. G. Jung into this category.

For category two, which he calls the de facto theist, there is "a very high probability but short of 100 per cent". It is important to notice that he does not say explicitly what this probability refers to.

He then goes on to give another eight categories. This is very interesting. Dawkins is very slippery when it comes to the idea of probability and he seems to use it in whatever way he chooses to at the time. Let's think carefully about what he has actually done here. First of all, he puts everybody into ten categories which indicate *how strongly they believe in God.* He then assigns these categories percentages relating to how certain the people in that category are that God exists; the first category being 100 percent certain that God exists. But that is not what Dawkins says. He says '*100 per cent probability of God*', which, you may have noticed, is not very clear. Why doesn't he say '*100 per cent sure that God exists*'? '100 percent probability of God' is ambiguous. By the time we get down to category four he is saying "exactly 50 per cent" and that God's existence and non-existence are 'equiprobable'.

Can you see what he has done? The 50 percent no longer relates to somebody being *50 percent sure that God exists*; it now means that God has a *50 percent probability of existing.* This is very deceptive.

Let me give you a Derren Brown example that is similar. Take, for example, his 'guessing which hand the coin is in' trick. Some people think he does this using only psychology (observing your eye movements, how you hold your hands out etc.); I'll call those people 100 percent believers. However, some people think he is purely cheating (in other words, he has a little electronic metal detector up his sleeve or something like that); I'll call them 0 percent believers. Some people may believe that he uses a mixture of both methods (maybe he only uses the metal detector when he's not sure – I don't know – it's not the greatest example but it will do); they will form the categories in between. Whatever category you are in, does it affect how Derren Brown is actually doing the trick? Of course, it doesn't affect it at all. If you are in the middle category because you are a 50 percent believer in Derren's psychological skills, it does not mean that there is a 50 percent chance that Derren is using psychology alone to guess which hand the coin is in. He's either cheating or he isn't, no matter what you think he's doing.

If you were to put it like this though, it would be altogether different. Let's say we were able to go back in time to before Derren had invented his coin in the hand trick. If we were to say, 'Given that Derren Brown is a magician, what is the probability that he will choose to use a method that is based on pure psychology?' Now we can start to say something meaningful, but remember that this is *not* what we are saying when it comes to God's existence. We can't talk about the Christian God and say, let's imagine going back in time to before God existed; now what are the chances of him coming into existence? This is what Richard Dawkins would like to be able to do, but you simply can't. As soon as you say that, you are no longer talking about the Christian God, because the Christian God *does not come into existence*. I'm sorry but he just doesn't play that game. You'll have to come up with something better.

The Biased Sample

A biased sample is one that is falsely presented as typical cross-section of the population from which it is drawn. For example, someone saying, 'Everyone liked *The God Delusion*' might fail to mention that the 'everyone' was actually made up only of Richard Dawkins' extended family and a few select members of the American Atheists Society.

In television magic shows there are several ways you can use biased samples. Firstly, you can be selective about what you show. Let us suppose that, like David Blaine did (to switch magicians for moment), I was going to make a television magic show and I decided to include the following trick. I go up to a random person on the street, try my best to look mysterious, and say slowly in a low voice, "I want you to think of a number between 1 and 50. Both of the digits must be different. Both of the digits must be odd numbers." I paused for a moment to read their mind before asking them, "Is it 37?"

If it is 37 and the person reacts by screaming hysterically, then this will probably make it into the programme. If they say no, their number was 13, then most of the time that footage will just end up on the cutting room floor, and the magician will simply ask somebody else to think of a number – but interestingly, not always. Sometimes being shown to occasionally get it wrong can add to your credibility, because it implies that you are not using foolproof magical methods. I mean, if you were a real mind reader you would get it wrong sometimes, wouldn't you? When you read a book, you occasionally misread a word, don't you? Surely you're not ashamed to admit that?

The sample could also be biased with respect to whom you choose to perform your magic. A performer will want to choose somebody who they think will give the right sort of reaction to their magic. Derren Brown brilliantly turns this on its head and uses it to his advantage by making the selection of 'suitable people' part of the trick. He makes it appear that it *does* matter who is chosen because his methods rely on him using the right sort of people, when most probably, in reality, most of the tricks would work with almost anyone. What it does though is make him look extra clever because not only is he about to read somebody's mind, but he can also tell very quickly what sort of a person somebody is just by asking them a few mundane questions. It really is great to watch.

In order to create his straw man version of religion in his television programme *Root of All Evil?*, Richard Dawkins seems to use a particularly biased sample of people who are mostly a little bizarre to say the least (and the same can be said of the odd collection of characters Derren Brown has included at the end of *Tricks of the Mind*, who have all e-mailed him asking him things such as if he would like to go round to their house for tea to discuss mind-reading). As Alister McGrath puts it, in his book, *The Dawkins Delusion*

> "One of the most characteristic features of Dawkins' anti-religious polemic is his presentation of the pathological as if it were normal, the fringe as if it were the centre, crackpots as if they were mainstream."[44]

They certainly do not appear to be an unbiased cross-section of the religious community. It is interesting to note that one of the people interviewed during the making of *Root of All Evil?* was Alister McGrath himself. However, his contribution did not make it into the final programme. It would appear he did not say 37.

The False or Shifted Dichotomy
Sometimes called a false dilemma, a false dichotomy is a situation in which two or more alternative points of view are treated as if they were the only options available, when in

reality there exists at least one more option which has not been considered.

In *The God Delusion*, Richard Dawkins asks why it is so important to God that we should believe in him? Why is this the one thing we should do? Why shouldn't he reward us because we are kind, generous or humble people?[45]

This is quite a clever thing to say. Let's think about it carefully. Firstly, it tries to say that you have these various different options; you can believe, or you can be kind, or you can be generous and so on, and Dawkins asks the question with the words *what is the one thing you must do?*, using the Kellogg's Cornflakes Suggestion perfectly, so that while we are thinking *what is the one thing?*, we have let the presupposition 'that there is only one thing' slip by unnoticed. In *The God Delusion*, the dichotomy is presented with six options; belief, kindness, generosity, humility, sincerity, and honest truth-seeking. It is, however, a false dichotomy. Belief in God is something that should inspire you to be all of these good things. The apostle John said, "The man who says, 'I know him,' but does not do what he commands is a liar" (1 John 2:4) and Jesus commands us to love our neighbour as we love ourselves. The book of James says that "faith without deeds is useless" (James 2:20). There are not various different options from which we can choose the one by which we think that God will accept us. Ultimately, God accepts us because of what Jesus did, not because of anything we do – the Bible says that even the ability to believe in him is a gift from God.

Again, the Kellogg's Cornflakes Suggestion is played beautifully when he asks why we so readily accept that the one thing we must do is believe. In the process of considering why we readily accept the idea, we fail to notice that the idea 'that we should and do readily accept the idea' is false. The Bible again makes this clear. James 2:19 says, "You believe that there is one God. Good! Even the demons believe that – and shudder." We need to do more than simply believe that God exists. To be a believer in Christ, we must also act in a way that somebody who really did believe in Christ would act. It is how we know that we really do believe. Belief in a biblical sense is not a passive thing.

Another thing you can do in order to mislead somebody is take a real dichotomy and move it to another place. I will call this a 'shifted dichotomy'. You can do some great things with this. If we look in *The God Delusion* at chapter seven we find a section called 'What about Hitler and Stalin? Weren't they atheists?' In this section, Dawkins tries to argue that Hitler and Stalin did not do evil things *because* they were atheists. It's rather an odd little section of the book. On page 273, Dawkins says that it doesn't matter whether Hitler and Stalin were atheists or not. Then he spends the next five pages trying to work out whether Hitler and Stalin were atheists, before concluding that Stalin was an atheist and Hitler probably wasn't.

In Christianity there is a very definite division drawn between two groups of people and in the end, the Bible says, it is the only division that matters. This division is between Christians and non-Christians; it is not between people who believe in God and people who don't believe in God. The Bible is quite clear about this, but by shifting the distinction from Christians and non-Christians to theists and atheists, you can do great things like, for example, putting Hitler and Christians into the same category. Furthermore, even if Hitler did not believe in God, Christians are in the same category as Hitler and Stalin, because they all had something they believed in that they were prepared to fight about. Atheists can then be proud because they would never go to war for the sake of an absence of belief.[46]

But surely Richard Dawkins is not here saying that we should never believe anything so strongly that we think it worth going to war over? Would he not believe in going to war to fight against evil people like Hitler and Stalin? No Christian I know is proud about the way that their religion has been abused by people looking for an excuse to start a fight. However, I believe that the Christian writer J. Gresham Machen was probably right when he said

> "In the sphere of religion, as in other spheres, the things about which men are agreed are apt to be the things that are least worth holding; the really important things are the things about which men will fight."[47]

The Argument from Personal Incredulity

In his book, *River out of Eden*, Richard Dawkins explains what he means by the Argument from Personal Incredulity.

> "Never say, and never take seriously anyone who says, 'I cannot believe that so-and-so could have evolved by gradual selection.' I have dubbed this kind of fallacy 'the Argument from Personal Incredulity.' Time and again, it has proven the prelude to an intellectual banana-skin experience."[48]

On the surface, this sounds fairly reasonable. It is similar to what Derren Brown says in *Tricks of the Mind*, when he says that to decide that the whole universe operates in a certain way, we should have a better argument than just 'It's true because I really, really feel it is.'[49]

It seems that Richard Dawkins is saying, "Don't disbelieve something just because you really, really feel it's not true," and Derren Brown is saying, "Don't believe something just because you really, really feel it *is* true." In other words, don't put too much trust in how you feel about something. Surely the correct way of approaching this kind of question is to ask what evidence there is to make you feel the way you do about something.

But does Richard Dawkins ever commit this fallacy himself? On page 55 of *The God Delusion*, Dawkins quotes Stephen Jay Gould from his book *Rock of Ages*.

"To say it for all my colleagues and for the umpteenth millionth time (from college bull sessions to learned treatises): science simply cannot (by its legitimate methods) adjudicate the issue of God's possible superintendence of nature. We neither affirm nor deny it; we simply can't comment on it as scientists."[50]

and on page 57 of *The God Delusion* we find Dawkins saying

"I simply do not believe that Gould could possibly have meant much of what he wrote in Rock of Ages."[51]

This sounds very much like the 'argument from personal incredulity' on Dawkins' part. What better evidence could Gould have left about what he believed than his own words in his own book? Yet Dawkins chooses to ignore this evidence because he just can't believe what Gould has written. It just goes to show that no matter what the evidence looks like, people will interpret it in the light of their own presuppositions.

The Use of Stooges

Derren Brown's television series *Trick of the Mind* begins with him saying, "This programme fuses magic, suggestion, psychology, misdirection and showmanship. I achieve the results you'll see through a varied mixture of those techniques. At no point are actors or stooges used in the show."[52] I often wonder what to make of these words. If we take it for granted that any magic programme essentially consists of lies and deception from start to finish, is this statement meant to be the one exception to this rule? Obviously, when the effects achieved seem too good to be true, the idea that stooges were used will occur to most people, and Derren will want to dismiss this from the outset if at all possible. Why wouldn't he use them though, if all he has in mind is how the trick will appear to the viewer? What difference does the method make? I have already suggested that methods involving 'invisible compromise' often result in the spectator not appearing quite as astonished as you might expect. So why not just get a good actor? In fact, you don't even need a good actor to pretend to fall asleep in a telephone box. I'm sure any old actor can fall over.

Derren Brown has said that the question of whether to use stooges is not a moral one, but an aesthetic one.[53] Can we not therefore conclude that if it made sense aesthetically, he would use stooges? I remember reading an interview once where he said that if he were to use stooges it would be too risky, as all one of them would have to do is own up to it and his show would be ruined. There is, obviously, some sense in this. I also remember though, reading something posted on the (always reliable, of course) Internet where somebody pretty much claimed just that. She said she had been at an audition along with the cab driver who couldn't remember where the London Eye was, even when he was looking right at it.[54] It was all very confusing, but here's another question. If we assume she was telling the truth (which, of course, she may well not have been), would that actually make her a stooge? What exactly constitutes a stooge? It's not a very clear concept when you think about it. I suppose it could be defined as somebody who is one of the performers pretending to be one of the spectators; but it's not even that clear cut. There is in magic the concept of the 'instant stooge'. This is somebody who starts out as a spectator but, part way through the trick, finds out what is really going on and, from that point on, plays along with the magician. Derren Brown suggests that many of his tricks involve hypnosis, and that when someone performs in a particular way under hypnosis, on a certain level many of them are just playing along with the performer.[55] How is that significantly different from using a stooge? Perhaps I am missing something obvious here. It's certainly one of the great many mysteries that surround Derren's act, and in a way there's a part of me that is glad I don't know the answer (though not a very big part of me). I'm not going to spend any more time speculating about it, because it will get me nowhere. What I am going to say is this; whether Derren Brown uses stooges or not, I just don't know. What I do know though is that Richard Dawkins uses them all the time. He just can't get enough of them.

A stooge is 'the enemy within'. They are somebody you think is on your side, but really they are on the other side. For us Christians this is a constant problem. How do we know who is really one of us? It's not obvious at all. Take, for example, this excerpt from a review of Dawkins' book *A Devil's Chaplain*.

> "This is the best book of sermons I have read for years. So please go on preaching to us, Reverend Dawkins, and don't mind the things they throw at you. After all, prophets always get stoned."

This review appeared in *The Guardian* on February 15th 2003. Who do you think would write something like that? That little excerpt, by the way, appears on the back cover of the paperback version (the version that I happen to own) of *A Devil's Chaplain*. Underneath it is the name of the man who wrote it. His name is Richard Holloway and he is, believe it or not, the former Bishop of Edinburgh. What are we to make of all this? Why would a Christian say something as bizarre as that about a book by Richard Dawkins? I decided to investigate this further. Here is another excerpt from the same review.

> "The goal of life is life itself. There is no final purpose, no end other than entropy and the end of all endings. But there is deep refreshment to be had "from standing up full-face into the keen wind of understanding". As a recovering Christian, I want to say amen to that, as well as adding a few final notes and quibbles."

A recovering Christian. That's an interesting phrase, don't you think? I think it implies that on some level he still considers himself to be a Christian; but he's recovering.

94

Recovering from what exactly? Well, it would appear that he is recovering from a lifetime of believing in Christianity. If you think this is strange, then you haven't heard anything yet. I logged on to Richard Dawkins' website and did a search for Richard Holloway. What I found was an article entitled *Atheists for Jesus*. In this article Richard Dawkins talks about Bishop Holloway, who has "evidently outgrown the supernaturalism which most Christians still identify with their religion." The article ends by seeming to suggest that if Jesus were to return today, he would be so appalled at what was being done in his name that he would "see through supernaturalist obscurantism" and himself become an atheist.

Richard Holloway is, I'm afraid, typical of the kind of 'Christian' Richard Dawkins loves to quote in order to make his points. They are simply stooges. Why don't we ever find Dawkins quoting Alister McGrath, Don Carson, Ravi Zacharias, Chuck Missler, Phillip Johnson, John MacArthur, Norman Geisler or even Philip Yancey? Oh yes, of course, because they don't say stupid things. What we get instead are things like this.

On page 17 of *The God Delusion*, the 'president of a historical society in New Jersey' is quoted as saying, "As everyone knows, religion is based on Faith, not knowledge." We have someone from Oklahoma telling Einstein to "go back to Germany where you came from." On page 35 we have Pope John Paul II saying that 'Our Lady of Fatima' altered the trajectory of a bullet from the gun of one of his would-be assassins. We have, on page 62, physicist Russell Stannard performing double-blind experiments on hospital patients to attempt to scientifically prove that people who are prayed for will recover more quickly than people who are not prayed for (even though God has made it perfectly clear that we are not to put him to the test – he doesn't play that game). On page 64 we have 'one of Britain's leading theologians' Richard Swinburne saying, "Some people badly need to be ill for their own sake, and some people badly need to be ill to provide important choices for others," which surely says more about the state of theology in Britain than it does about Christianity. All of these comments pale into insignificance though when compared with the appalling things found on page 211 to 213. I won't repeat any of them here; suffice to say, they almost make you feel as though Richard Dawkins might have a point – and, surely, that precisely *is* the point.

It doesn't take an intellect like Richard Dawkins' to mock such nonsense. The point is that this is not Christianity. Whether these people are insane, misguided or simply misquoted, they are stooges, and they are being used by a clever performer to produce a desired effect. Don't fall for it. If you want to find out what Christians really believe, it should go without saying that you're probably not going to discover it within the pages of a book called *The God Delusion*.

Telling the Truth

This is another method that can be used to cause confusion. If somebody is expecting, or half-expecting, to be tricked, then telling the truth can be a great option. Mixing truth with lies is regularly used to great effect by both Derren Brown and Richard Dawkins.

5. A Devil's Commentary

The Magic of Richard Dawkins

If Christianity is true, then much of what is written in *The God Delusion* must be false. If Richard Dawkins' aim is that religious readers who open the book will be atheists when they put it down, then for this ever to succeed, the reader must be tricked into accepting a false worldview. If the reader is to be tricked, then we might expect to be able to work out how this trick is done by carefully reading the book, with all the sleights from the previous chapters in mind.

I'd like to make it very clear from the outset that this chapter in my book is a work of fiction. What it consists of is my attempt to explain how the trick that is *The God Delusion* could have been done. As with much of the magic of Derren Brown, how it actually was done must remain something of a mystery. In a sense this chapter can be viewed as simply me having a bit of fun, playing with the ideas outlined in the previous chapters. I have written much of it in a tongue-in-cheek manner and I do not intend any of it to be taken too seriously. At the same time though, I am trying to make some serious points here, and my main attitude towards Richard Dawkins and *The God Delusion* is always one of concern not only for his own soul, but for the souls of all the other countless people who read his book and are affected by it. If I can prevent even one person from becoming an atheist as a result of reading *The God Delusion* then writing this book will have been a worthwhile exercise.

I have decided, as with most explanations of magic, to write this chapter from the point of view of a magician. By this I do not mean to pretend to write from the point of view of Richard Dawkins; rather I am writing as if I were someone, or something, far more malevolent. For this reason, God will be referred to as 'the enemy', what most people consider to be good will be treated as though it were bad, and so on. From the narrator's point of view, 'my scribe' obviously refers to

Richard Dawkins himself. Most of us by now are familiar with the idea of a DVD commentary. This chapter can be thought of in a similar way. It would be helpful to have a copy of *The God Delusion* with you, as I will be referring to specific page numbers in the margin of my text. Again, for this, I will be using the British first edition hardback version of the book.

As with anybody who tries to explain somebody else's magic, I will probably be wrong a lot of the time. However, I hope to be right at least some of the time too, and even when I am not, I hope that I will have occasionally given you something to think about. If you are a Christian, maybe you would like to take another book by another atheist and try to work out how their trick was done. I rather like the idea of 'devil's commentaries' being written for many anti-Christian books. It seems to me to be an unexplored genre with a lot of potential.

At the very least, I hope this chapter keeps you suitably entertained; after all, isn't that what magic is meant to be all about?

Preface

1   The great magician Eugene Burger once said that magic does not begin when you begin the first trick; it begins the moment you introduce yourself. In a similar way, when constructing a book designed to deceive, the Preface is important, as I think it sets the tone of the work and aims to put the reader into the correct frame of mind right from the outset. The magic does not start with chapter 1; it starts here, and the message is simple. Religion is bad; atheism is good. I tried to enforce this by saying that atheism is 'realistic', 'splendid', 'brave' and atheists can be 'happy', 'balanced', 'moral' and 'intellectually fulfilled.' Once we have said these things, we can say something about religion.

I think it works to appeal to the reader's emotions. When they think of religion, I want them to think of suicide bombers flying planes into the World Trade Center. I want them to transfer all of their hatred for the 9/11 hijackers to religion in general, even though as we know most religious people are, relatively speaking, good people. I really don't want to let religion conjure up images of characters such as Ned Flanders from *The Simpsons*. This would not be a good way to start.

Now, I know that not everybody will fall for the 'all religious people are like 9/11 hijackers' nonsense (although many will), so here's what I did next. Bombard them with a list of any evil people or events from history that are even remotely connected with religion. The usual ones work best; the Crusades obviously (one of my favourites), the troubles in Northern Ireland, greedy televangelists etc. It wasn't difficult to come up with quite a good list. What we are doing here though is 'shifting the dichotomy.' Let me explain, because this is great. As we know, all the people in the world, as far as the enemy is concerned, are divided into two groups; those who are called Christians (by which he means those who have entered into a relationship with him through his son, Jesus), and those who are not in such a relationship. Fortunately for us, we have made sure that this distinction is often blurred in the 'real world' that we have created and control, and it is often difficult for people to know who belongs in which category. Even better for us, in a book such as *The God Delusion*, we can go one step further and pretend that the real division is not between Christians and non-Christians, but between 'religious' people and 'non-religious' people. This makes our job much easier because we can group real Christians together with people like the Muslim suicide bombers and the Taliban. Christians can easily be made to appear 'guilty by association' and this is even before we get to the bottom of the first page.

2 The next move is one that I am particularly proud of, and it will work extremely well with a particular kind of person. It makes me smile to even think about it. Tell them that religious people (I know this sounds silly) would even change the lyrics to one of John Lennon's songs. This sort of thing can have a very interesting effect on certain people. Don't forget that for some people, John Lennon is literally a god. Remember when Andy Warhol spoke of this effect in his philosophy book? He said that he was approached by a company who wanted to purchase his 'aura'.[1] He said he didn't know what they really meant – but how would he, as this is another of our inventions? For somebody to have an aura is for them to represent something transcendent. In other words, they take the place of the enemy. We have now achieved this to such a degree with the class of humans called

'celebrities' that it amazes even me. People like John Lennon though, who die relatively young, often have a tremendous aura. To blaspheme him has the same effect on many people as blaspheming the enemy has on Christians.

2-3   The next section, the remainder of page 2 and most of page 3, is all about being confident. I make it sound as though the trick I am about to perform is a very easy one. I suggest to the reader that the arguments I am about to make have, in effect, already been made. Remember that most of my readers are on my side, but in case there are any readers who are not convinced yet, this is what I do.

3   I start, every now and then, to tell the truth. I know it's not a pleasant experience but it works wonders. For example, many Christians would agree that there is probably technically no such thing as a 'Christian child' and we know this, but it sounds quite plausible to them that we might think that they thought such a thing actually existed (indeed, as we know, some religious people really do believe this – something to do with covenants, I think they say). Try it yourself. Before you know it, you will have many readers agreeing with you. In fact, because they also get annoyed at such terminology, they will positively warm to you, often to the extent that when you start lying again they will be far more inclined to take what you have to say seriously.

5   It's not only people who can possess an aura. Sometimes books can too. This is definitely the case when it comes to *Zen and the Art of Motorcycle Maintenance*. It's a great book, and if you can make it sound as though a book like this is 'on your side' you win over all the people who liked that book.

Another thing you can try, which many people will fall for, is to *dare them to read your book.* Say something like, 'of course, most Christians will be warned not to read books like this.' Some people just can't resist a dare! Of course, it is quite sensible for many Christians, especially the inexperienced, to not read books like this. I mean, who would send people out into a battle without the proper equipment? Many will certainly not be prepared for this kind of spiritual warfare and, with any luck, we will win many souls in this way.

6   A subtle touch of irony, just before you give the usual list of people you wish to thank, would be to openly thank our father below, who is, of course, ultimately responsible for all works such as these. It is by him that all of the sleights we have used so far were created.

A Deeply Religious Non-believer

11   **Deserved Respect.** This chapter is very important. Its aim is to confuse while appearing to clarify, and hopefully bring the reader subtly around to our way of thinking, so that by the time we reach the next chapter, where it starts to get serious, they will be on our side.

        Notice how on this page I use the word 'decent' to refer to a liberal clergyman, seemingly in passing. This sort of 'defining words to suit our own purposes' is very valuable and very deceptive. If it goes by unnoticed, it will start to reshape the way the reader perceives things.

12-13   In order to hide this process, we will pretend that our aim is to actually clarify what words mean. Here I question somebody's use of the word 'religion' and on the next page question somebody else's use of the word 'God'. Here I quote somebody saying that 'God' can be given any meaning that we like, which is something the majority of my readers will agree with, I'm sure. The clever part, though, is that I say it as if I believe they would disagree with me. This makes the reader think to themselves, "Hang on, I agree with you here. Maybe I'm going to agree with a lot more things that you say. You and I may not be all that different, you know. All of this may be some sort of great misunderstanding!" If we can achieve this effect, then we are winning. Then I go on to clarify another word just to force the point home, so to speak. With any luck, the reader will be so wrapped up in their agreement with us that they will not notice what I do at the start of the next page.

14   Here I actually make a true statement about what atheists believe, but I imply more than I actually say. After declaring the materialistic worldview, I say that thoughts and emotions *emerge* from a complex brain. Do I say how they emerge? Do I *know* how they emerge in this way? Well, of course, they don't emerge in this way at all, but I make it look as though I do know (and I love this) by writing the word emerge in italics! It is no longer 'emerge' – it is *'emerge'*. The emphasis acts almost like magic – it's as if somebody has asked me, "How do these things emerge?" and I say, "Don't you know? They just *emerge!*" You can almost feel these things *emerging* as you read the word. We laughed about this one for hours when we came up with it.

14 –
16   Here I make the point that many scientists (including Albert Einstein, Stephen Hawking, and Robert Winston) are all atheists (or as good as), as if this is important. It isn't really. I criticise them for using the words 'God' and 'religion' in figurative ways, as

it may give the wrong impression (I, of course, will use words such as 'design', 'engineer' and 'good' in similarly figurative ways that equally annoy the enemy's followers but that's another matter!).

16   Here I take the opportunity to declare two of my favourite repeated ideas, just in passing. These are that theology is not a real subject and that the idea of God is analogous to the idea of fairies (this analogy is obviously false as many people come to believe in God as adults, and this cannot really be said of fairies). It is all leading up to something very important.

16 - 17   Bring on the stooges! The first is an American Roman Catholic lawyer. I love doing this. Why should we have to keep attacking the enemy when they seem so perfectly happy to attack themselves? I always use a stooge when I want to quote somebody from the enemy's camp, as a way of misrepresenting Christianity. I can then very easily make the enemy look 'silly by association'. This is a simple matter of exploiting the ignorance of the reader, who will usually take the stooge to be fairly representing the enemy's position. Because with this technique you can literally work wonders, you will see me use it time after time after time.

20 - 27   **Undeserved Respect**. Here I am using the same general techniques that I have already employed. I begin by quoting Douglas Adams, who has a tremendous aura, as one of our spokespeople. I then spend the remainder of the chapter saying things that most of our readers will agree with. I mention things that I don't like (such as certain kinds of religious extremism), in the knowledge that they too will not like them. I am witty at times. By the end of this section, many readers will feel as though I have a lot

to say that is worth listening to. Some of the things they themselves will have been thinking, and in many ways they will be glad that somebody like myself has finally said them. Hopefully, they may even feel that they are starting to actually like me. And that is when I hit them!

The God Hypothesis

31   Just when I have the reader on side, I launch an all out attack on 'The God of the Old Testament'. I call him everything I can possibly imagine. Then I quote Churchill's (aura) son to bang the final nail into the coffin. Then I attack Jesus. Then I say that I am not attacking any particular God – but I just have! This is actually quite clever as well as very funny. My scribe would not attack Allah in a similar way because this would be too dangerous. The Christian God can be attacked in perfect safety because Christians will not retaliate. Now think about what I have just said. *Christians will not retaliate.* So I can take advantage of this reality to attack their God whenever I want to, but then accuse *all religions* of being equally violent, and so on, whenever I want to. Hardly anyone notices this! Also, I get to actually attack Allah (and Baal, Wotan etc – they don't matter – nobody knows who they are – they're just a diversion) by saying that I am *not attacking* 'any god in particular'. In other words I *am* attacking all gods, but make it sound like I'm attacking *none* of them!

Now I take advantage of an off-beat (while people are still recovering from the 'attack by not attacking') to do something that is both good and bad, as far as our purposes are concerned. I introduce a straw man god. I try not to make it too obvious, but I admit I could have probably done better than this. I mention a god who 'comes into existence' as a process of 'gradual evolution'. I conclude that this god is a delusion because a complex god, necessarily arriving late in the universe, could not have designed the universe. I do say god 'in this sense defined' but, even as I say it, I know that nobody apart from spirits like myself, would ever dream of defining god in this way. The problem I really have is that by defining god in a way that is general enough to represent *no god in particular* (and at the same time all particular gods), he actually becomes *no god at all*. It is also an unfortunate part of the book where my scribe's presupposed evolutionary beliefs really shine through (remember, many of the enemy's people have not bought into this). They have to though, as this is what he is best known for, but the problem is, once you define a god in this way, it is certainly not the Christian God. You just have to hope that this one goes by unnoticed.

32   To reinforce this idea of a god who comes into existence, I use a bit of evolutionary pseudo-history at the top of the next page. The belief in Darwinian evolution is something you can really take advantage of. Although I've said that many Christians will not accept this theory, many of your readers (including many Christians) will. Many people who do believe it will automatically want to apply it to everything, and even if they don't, you can apply it to everything and many of them will just accept whatever you say. Here I use the half-truth method. I mention that historians of religion recognise a progression from tribal animism to polytheisms to monotheisms. What I don't mention is that most of these historians lived in the nineteenth century, and most of today's historians do not believe this at all, due to all sorts of archaeological evidence that does not work in our favour.

| 32 – | **Polytheism.** Red herrings and ridicule are the order |
| 36 | of the day here, guaranteed to stifle any thoughts that |

32 –
36
Polytheism. Red herrings and ridicule are the order of the day here, guaranteed to stifle any thoughts that the reader may have been having during the previous section. If you want to try this yourself, just write down the first things that come into your head. Anything generally negative about religion will do. Never question whether the perpetrators of whatever crimes you discuss were acting in accordance with their religion or not. It's irrelevant. All we are doing is trying to create a mood before we launch our next attack.

34 -
35
Here I pick an easy target by discussing the doctrine of the Trinity. Because this concerns the very nature of the enemy, it can be quite difficult to comprehend (in fact, we don't understand it any more than Christians do really, if the truth be told – but obviously it shouldn't be). Christians have been faced with these kinds of problems for thousands of years. None of them really understands the Trinity. However, one thing that Christians down through the centuries have had to do is write things down for future generations. So how do you go about writing something down when you don't really understand the thing you are writing about? Fortunately for us, the answer is often very badly, which is just what we require in order to perform the following trick.

This is what I do; I quote Thomas Jefferson, the third president of the United States. This is a lesson really worth learning. If you quote somebody who sounds important saying something that sounds clever, people will believe anything, because they will not stop and think things through. Here is the quotation that I relate to the idea of the Trinity.

"Ridicule is the only weapon which can be used

against unintelligible propositions. Ideas must
be distinct before reason can act upon them; and
no man ever had a clear idea of the trinity. It is
the mere Abracadabra of the mountebanks
calling themselves the priests of Jesus."[2]

Surely he must be right? He's used lots of long words
and he was President of the United States of America
– you're probably safer not quoting any of the more
recent presidents! With regard to how this statement
creates the desired effect then; obviously, it is not
clear here what is meant to be 'unintelligible'; is it the
Trinity itself or somebody's attempt to describe it. If I
mean the attempt to describe it, then this does not
imply that the Trinity itself is unintelligible. If I mean
that the Trinity itself is unintelligible, then surely I
would expect somebody's attempt to describe it to be
equally unintelligible, or wrong. Either way,
somebody's attempt to describe the Trinity does not
necessarily tell me anything about the Trinity at all.
Secondly, to say that 'no man ever had a clear idea of
the Trinity' is, to be honest, which I'm not going to
make a habit of being so don't get used to it, quite
bizarre. For any human to have a clear understanding
of what any other human thinks about anything at all
is difficult enough. To claim to know that no human
anywhere has ever had a clear idea of what something
is, even if this something is as mysterious as the
Trinity, is quite something. Jefferson was most
probably under the illusion (and remember that
illusions are our business), as many people are, that if
he couldn't understand something, then *nobody* else
could either. That's why he was the President!
Obviously this is just my attempt at an argument from
authority.

I used this quote not because I thought it was clever,
but rather because I found it quite amusing. What
Jefferson appears to have done is be deliberately

unclear in the way he has used the word 'clear'! Is it true that Christians have *no clear ideas* of the Trinity? Well, of course they do. The Trinity consists of three distinct persons with their own personalities. That is a clear idea. It is simply not true for Jefferson to say that just because an entity is mysterious and he doesn't fully understand how it is put together and he doesn't fully understand how it thinks, that he does not have *any clear ideas* about such an entity. The above description could probably be applied by most men to their wives! On top of this, again and again emphasise that unless you can *reason*, you can do nothing. Don't let them worry about the fact that not even this statement itself can be arrived at using reason alone without the reasoning being circular. It doesn't matter. Most readers are on our side! They want to be tricked.

Suggesting, as I do, that the Trinity really implies 'a monotheism that is really a polytheism' consisting of three gods means that I can attack Christianity both in the polytheism and monotheism sections of my book! This 'trinity is really three gods' idea has been a common misconception held by people of other religions for many centuries and a personal favourite of mine. To move the argument (if you can call it that) into the, in reality, sometimes rather strange beliefs of the Roman Catholic church with regard to Mary and the saints, gives the impression that the Trinity, as an idea, is 'silly by association' (the association fallacy is quite versatile and you should try to use it whenever possible). I thought even I was pushing my luck a little when I suggested that the Pope (who acted as a good stooge here, by the way) had 'polytheistic hankerings' but it's all meant to be in good humour isn't it, in a sort of deadly-serious kind of way.

36   Another attempt to clear things up for the reader by confusing them. I claim to decry supernaturalism in all its forms, but *for convenience' sake* I will focus on the most familiar form of this supernaturalism, namely (although obviously I *don't* name him) the God of the Bible. At the bottom of the same page I say that I am not attacking any one god, but all gods. This is obviously a contradiction. To mask this, I insert a section in between. I know that I am going to be accused of setting up a straw man god (because I am). The way I choose to get out of this is to set up a straw straw man. I will set up the 'man with the white beard', knock him down myself, then replace him with… well, no god in particular because how could I? That would be far too specific. I just refer to supernaturalism in general. As long as I have not defined here the god I am referring to, the reader can just assume that I have (hopefully they may have already forgotten that definition I gave previously of a god who 'comes into existence' – it is a bit of an embarrassment) and that it happens to be their god.

37   **Monotheism.** Here I use my dichotomy shift again when I mention that I will treat all the Abrahamic religions as one and the same thing. I also mention that I will not consider Buddhism and Confucianism as being religions but rather 'philosophies of life'. My motive for this (not obvious, I hope) is that by defining what a religion is in this way, I can avoid the rather obvious accusation that atheism itself is a religion.

38   On this page I just have another dig at the enemy by stating that he has human qualities, when we know very well that it is the other way around. This is an example of evidence that could be interpreted either way depending upon your presuppositions. I naturally present them in terms of the atheist's presuppositions.

Remember to always assume your conclusions up front.

38 -   **Secularism, the Founding Fathers and the Religion**
42   **of America.** Here I talk about how the Founding
        Fathers of America were atheists of sorts. It's a bit of
        a jumble of ideas really (I think I must have let my
        scribe's mind wander a little – was this the day I got
        called away on another assignment? I don't know). I
        remember the next Jefferson quote.

42   Good old Thomas Jefferson. Such eloquent nonsense.
        In this age of style over substance, these sound bites
        are priceless. *To talk of immaterial things is to talk of
        nothings.* Utterly meaningless, but *so* plausible to the
        non-thinking reader. Not even many materialists
        would go this far. So are there no such things as
        'propositions' then, for example? In his last quote
        Jefferson actually talked about 'propositions'. But is a
        proposition a material thing? No. So this means then
        that in this quotation Jefferson is saying that his
        previous quotation is meaningless. Isn't it great! I
        love him, I really do! *I cannot reason otherwise*, he
        says; the implication being 'therefore neither can
        anybody else.' Actually, this quotation contains
        something which was to be a bit of a recurring theme;
        namely the idea that there is *no evidence* for the
        supernatural. That's right; no evidence for me! Of
        course, by 'no evidence' they mean *'no evidence for
        which any materialistic theory whatsoever, no matter
        how far fetched, cannot be dreamed up'*. This is quite
        amusing to watch from our point of view. They have
        now reached the point that in order to avoid having to
        accept that the enemy is the best explanation for the
        universe (due to the anthropic principle) many of them
        are suggesting that an infinite number of parallel
        universes must exist! I almost feel redundant. As we
        know, *any materialistic theory at all* will be accepted

111

before a supernatural explanation will be considered, which means they will always come up with something they consider to be plausible – never mind the evidence; we just say we need that when it suits us. In fact, as you know, it is even better than that because of the principle of invisible compromise. The scientific method will never even consider a supernatural explanation for anything because it has been ruled out by definition. They would rather not know how something works than know that it is the enemy who makes it work. But do they mind? No, they 'exalt in ignorance'! You see, if they ever did arrive at the conclusion that a supernatural explanation was the best option, given the evidence, they would be guilty in their own eyes of the 'god of the gaps' fallacy and they would no longer be able to accuse the enemy's people of doing the same thing, so no matter how much evidence you give them for the enemy's existence, they will always want more. It is a similar situation to the one we have created with money, except this one costs us nothing. What *we* must never forget is that religious beliefs are highly complex. Often people will say one thing on one day and another thing on another. We just need to be there on the right day. Remember, our job is not to clarify. We must strive to make the complex appear simple and the simple appear complex. You'll get the hang of it.

43   Thomas Jefferson again. I use a false dichotomy here. The only two options are not really 'the homage of reason' or 'blindfolded fear', but I suppose it may fool some people.

44 -   Remember; *always* judge a philosophy by its abuse.[3]
45   Always, always, always. In this way you will be able to link any ideology with any action you desire. Of course, if anybody ever says to us something like

'Hitler was just being a good Darwinist trying to advance humanity by wiping out what he considered to be inferior races' we must always be very quick to point out that Hitler was *abusing* Darwin's ideas, not consistently following them through, although it always pays to be as sketchy as possible when attempting to explain exactly *how* he was abusing the ideas. Don't worry about it. People will never question you if you sound knowledgeable enough. Also, make use of shifted dichotomy whenever you can to lump all religions together. They immediately become easier to attack and more difficult to defend.

46   It is worth a comment that here I mention 'The God Hypothesis' properly for the first time. I also mention the enemy's improbability again, to which I will return later.   You may wonder what kind of a hypothesis 'The God Hypothesis' is? Is it a scientific hypothesis? This being the same science that rules out the enemy by definition? Don't worry if this confuses you. It's meant to. Confusion is good.

47 -   **The Poverty of Agnosticism.** Here I claim that
49   agnosticism is acceptable on questions where there is not enough evidence to decide either way, for example, whether there is life elsewhere in the universe.   I claim that the existence of God could warrant a 'temporary' kind of agnosticism, by which I mean that when we have enough evidence to decide on the question of God's existence, we need no longer be agnostic about it. A great technique in magic is to mix truth with deception. Much of the enjoyment gained from certain types of magic results from the spectator trying to work out where the truth ends and where the deception begins. Here is where my deception begins. I say that we need not be agnostic about the enemy because, although we cannot absolutely prove or disprove his existence, we can

113

show that he is *improbable* enough for us to conclude that he doesn't exist.

50 -
51

This is a great moment of magic. I begin by using the semi-attached figure in the following way. First of all, I put people into ten categories which indicate *how strongly they believe in God.* I then assign these categories percentages relating to how certain the people in that category are that God exists; the first category being 100 percent certain that God exists. But that is not what I say. I say '*100 per cent probability of God.*' Why don't I say, '*100 per cent sure*'? Because '100 percent probability of God' is ambiguous. By the time I get down to category four I am saying that both God's existence and his non-existence have an equal probability. Can you see what I have done? The 50 percent no longer relates to somebody being *50 percent sure that God exists*; it now means that God has a *50 percent probability of existing*. This is a routine that I am particularly proud of.

What will hopefully go unnoticed is that this god is the straw man god. I can't talk about the Christian God legitimately and say, let's imagine going back in time to before God existed (because we know that he created time); now what are the chances of him coming into existence? As soon as I say that, I am no longer talking about the Christian God, because the Christian God *did not and could not by definition come into existence.* Hardly anybody will question this however and it should be fairly straightforward to convince somebody that a god who actually doesn't exist probably doesn't exist.

52 –
54

All that now needs to be done is use my own definition of 'evidence' to show that there is no evidence at all for the enemy's existence, and therefore he is just as improbable as Bertrand Russell's orbiting teapot. From this I conclude that we should treat the enemy as if he didn't exist. That is how you prove atheism.

55 - 56 **NOMA.** Always try to have it both ways if at all possible. Here I ask why scientists should not be able to comment on God, whereas elsewhere I have stated that God can never be an acceptable scientific explanation of anything; so on the one hand I allow God, and on the other hand I don't.

I mention Stephen Jay Gould's false dichotomy NOMA (non-overlapping magisteria) which asserts that science explains why things work the way they do, but religion explains questions of ultimate meaning. I bring this up to show that I am a good logician and will not accept false dichotomies of this sort. I then bring in a falsehood of my own. I claim that the scientific questions are really the only questions that are valid, and that questions of ultimate meaning are themselves meaningless. How do I convince my reader of this obvious falsehood? I blind them with nonsense, using an 'argument by confusion.' Read the section from 'It is a tedious cliché...' to 'imply that religion can.' Can you make out any kind of argument there? That's because there is not meant to be one. It's a sort of 'modern art' version of an argument. I then sum things up by saying that if science cannot answer a question, this does not imply that religion can. Hopefully they will be so confused at this point that they will believe the summing up simply out of sheer relief that finally they have come across a concept that makes sense to them. They won't bother to check if it's true or false.

56 – 57 Note that on both of these pages I have managed to reiterate my point that theology is not actually a real

subject. Hopefully, this idea will be slowly sinking in to the reader's mind.

57   I pull a fast one here and hope nobody will notice. I use my scribe's own 'argument from personal incredulity' when I say I do not believe that Stephen Jay Gould meant what he said in his book *Rock of Ages*. Hopefully, nobody will notice this inconsistency.

58   On this page I dismiss Richard Swinburne's definition of the Christian God by saying that it is 'just too easy'! What I mean to imply is that anything that seems 'just too easy' must therefore be false (with the exception of natural selection being responsible for everything imaginable). This sort of dismissal really is 'just too easy', but it seems to work.

59   Now I really go for it. I say that there is *no evidence* for God (yes, I know, it's silly but what else am I supposed to say?). How do I back this up? I say that if there were any evidence, apologists would immediately throw out NOMA (I am using the word 'evidence' here in my strictly 'scientific' way – discounting things like personal experience etc.). What I fail to mention however, is that hardly any apologists accept NOMA anyway. I am using the Kellogg's Cornflake Suggestion really, implying that they do accept it by discussing under what circumstances they would abandon it.

60 –   I end the section with a couple of standard techniques;
61   mockery and insult. I quote Ambrose Bierce's *Devil's Dictionary*, then shortly afterwards call God violent and clumsy.

61 -   **The Great Prayer Experiment** is a trick in itself, and
63   is one that I am really proud of. This is how it works.

First, say up front that the experiment to test prayer is amusing and pathetic. What you will be implying to most readers is that this is because prayer itself is amusing and pathetic, and this is before the trick has even begun.

Secondly, set up a straw man, reductionist version of prayer in order to be able to test it. The reductionism here is based on the fact that the experiment only really involves the people being prayed for and the people actually praying. Mention the enemy so that people do not get suspicious but be sure to treat prayer as a purely mechanical process where the request goes in and the results come out. As we know, the enemy does not operate in this mechanical way but has a personality. In real prayer, people make their requests known to him and he chooses in his 'wisdom' how to answer these requests. This is so obvious that in order to prevent even the most ignorant reader from simply dismissing this experiment as ridiculous, be sure to add plenty of extra details to make the experiment sound more credible. Mention things like the fact it was a 'double-blind' experiment, and go into a lot of detail about how the experiment was conducted. By the time the reader has attended to all of these red herrings, hopefully they will have forgotten that what we are dealing with here is not how real prayer works.

The next point is where the magic happens. All you do is quote somebody who is happy to mock these experiments. Here it helps if this person is a non-believer. In the process of mocking the ridiculous experiment, which is obviously deserving of mockery by both believers and non-believers, the inattentive reader will associate the mockery not with the silly experiment but with the whole idea of prayer itself. At this point you have achieved your aim.

You can further cement this idea in the mind of the reader by various means. Lots of mockery obviously – this always works. Try to find actual Christians (stooges) who are prepared to comment on these experiments *as if they were valid*. Failing that (or as well as that, if you are confident enough), find Christians who will condemn the experiments, and then find something stupid that they said that will seem to suggest that whatever they think, the opposite must be the true because they are so stupid.

It is worthy of note that another great scientist, Oliver Sacks, used this method not only to dismiss prayer but to dismiss the idea of God entirely. Remember that in his autobiography, *Uncle Tungsten*, he said

> "What evidence was there, I kept asking myself, for God's existence? At Braefield, I determined on an experiment to resolve the matter decisively: I planted two rows of radishes side by side in the vegetable garden, and asked God to bless one or curse one, whichever He wished, so that I might see a clear difference between them. The two rows of radishes came up identical, and this was proof for me that no God existed."[5]

Don't ever underestimate the power of this effect.

66 - 69 **The Neville Chamberlain School of Evolutionists.** Here's a great false analogy for you. I suggest that scientists who contribute towards a positive working relationship between science and religion are of the 'Neville Chamberlain' school. For those of you too young to remember Hitler personally, Neville Chamberlain was Prime Minister of Great Britain. In 1938, he attempted to avoid what was to become known as the 'second world war' by trying to appease Hitler. I suggest that scientists of the Neville

Chamberlain school are simply trying to appease religious people. The nice thing about this analogy is that as well as scientists being represented by Neville Chamberlain, religious people are represented by Hitler. Hopefully, this will give the (perhaps unconscious) impression to the reader that Christians are all like Hitler.

70 - 73 **Little Green Men.** Of course, I don't say anything at all about this in my book but this thing about SETI is very interesting. How do you know that the signal you have detected is a sign of intelligence? Our friend Carl Sagan suggested the detection of prime numbers in his novel *Contact*, since they could not, as far as we know, be produced by natural processes. One of our enemies made the observation that, "The irony lies in the fact that Sagan was absolutely convinced that a simple string of prime numbers proves the existence of an intelligent being, but the equivalent of 1,000 encyclopaedias in the first one-celled life does not. *It takes a lot of faith not to believe in God.*"[6] Now this is not 'god of the gaps' stuff; this is actual evidence for the enemy, and it does take an awful lot of faith not to believe in him, given evidence like this. Fortunately for us though, we've redefined the word 'evidence', redefined 'faith' and redefined 'God', so even this sort of thing can't touch us. This technique of redefining is like spiritual armour plating. I hope by now you are beginning to see the potential for deception that is available to you, simply by using a few basic techniques.

Arguments for God's Existence

77 - 79 **Thomas Aquinas' 'proofs'.** This section deals with arguments for God's existence and the aim is to discredit these arguments. It is important to

119

remember that I do not want to clarify issues for my reader, therefore my approach will *not* be a logical analysis of each argument, giving counter-arguments and the like. This would give the wrong impression entirely. If I did this it would seem that I am suggesting that these arguments deserve serious consideration. Whether they do or do not is utterly unimportant. I will simply treat them as though they do not. I will treat them all as if they have been disproved before I even start, and wherever possible I will simply ridicule them.

Let us consider first the arguments involving an infinite regress. It is important that *you* know that all that these arguments are really used for by Christians today is to point out that an infinite regress is a real problem that they have a possible solution to. What *I* claim though, to *my* reader, is that these arguments are meant to prove the existence of the Christian God entirely, along with all his terrible attributes. The truth, as far as we're concerned, is that an infinite regress *really is* a problem for us. Our best scientists have concluded that the universe, by which they mean the whole of time and space, *began* with a 'big bang'. They have no idea why or how. It is pointless to speak of anything before it, because time itself, remember, only came into existence at that point, so the concept of 'before' is meaningless. According to the enemy's people, he provides a good solution to this problem (which obviously he does because he is the solution) so what I do is *attack misconceptions*. I say that Christians make an *unwarranted* assumption that God is immune to regress. This is a dangerous move because, as you know, we are no strangers to unwarranted assumptions ourselves! What Christians might say is that God *must be* immune to regress in order for him to be a solution. This sounds delightfully like one of our own arguments.

120

However, the truth is more likely to be this. The idea of the enemy being immune to regress comes from somewhere else, for example, that *Book* of his. What Christians then do is the following. They assume the definition of the enemy from the *Book* to be true. Then they look at the evidence and see if it fits the story, and it does. A God who is immune to regress provides a convenient solution to this problem of regress. What they then do is say that given the problem of regress, such a God is a good hypothesis as far as a solution goes. Fortunately for us, this then gets mistakenly labelled as a 'proof', which nowadays has all sorts of mathematical overtones of certainty which we can exploit. You see, these arguments do all point to the enemy, but none of them are meant to be taken in isolation as absolute proof of his existence. The idea is that they are meant to have a cumulative effect. When you take one argument after the next after the next, they do point very strongly to the enemy. However, if you consider them in isolation, they are individually quite weak. Therefore, this is the approach we must take. Divide and conquer. Attack them *individually*. Ridicule them *individually* for their inefficiencies, always overstating the claims of each one, making them easy to knock down. See what I do at the bottom of the page. I say that even if there were anything to these arguments, there is no reason to ascribe to the enemy omnipotence, omniscience, goodness, and I reel off a whole list of these. Now, of course there is no reason to ascribe these attributes to the enemy based on these arguments (they have other arguments for these), but *nobody is claiming there is,* apart from me! After explaining this, I give a quote from an eminent philosopher – sorry, what am I saying, I quote Edward Lear, the famous writer of nonsense poetry to tie it all up before moving on to the next one.

121

The 'argument from degree' is a bit of a red herring. Nobody would use such an argument as a proof for the existence of God, since for one thing it is obviously circular in the given form. The idea that we judge goodness by comparing it with a maximum standard of goodness really presupposes the conclusion; namely, that this God whose character *is* the standard actually exists. I do not mention circularity, since this may draw attention to our own use of this method, but I do use the argument as an excuse to insult the enemy again. How I actually define what is 'good' apart from with reference to the enemy is a tricky issue, which I will 'deal with' in due course! The 'argument from degree' does serve a useful purpose though, as I would not like to put the regression arguments right next to the argument from design, as they both make quite strong points.

With the 'argument from design' I start with a blatant lie. I say that the argument from design is the only argument still in use today. It isn't, but remember the principle of isolation. If it *were* the only argument still in use, it would stand alone and therefore could be attacked alone. I deal with this argument very quickly – essentially I just say the magic word, which is of course 'Darwin'. Again, remember that the argument from design does not 'prove' the existence of the enemy; it simply says that if he existed and he did design his creatures, we should expect to see evidence of design, and we do. What Darwin actually did was provide us with exactly what we always need but don't always have; namely, *any remotely plausible sounding alternative to God*. We can then comfortably ignore the enemy in this area by applying the 'if it *could* have happened this way, then it *must* have happened this way' principle. They will always accept the 'most likely explanation' and, since according to our special definition of God, he is always the *least* likely explanation, Darwin wins!

80 - 85 **The ontological argument and other *a priori* arguments.** The whole trick here is to imply, by my complete lack of engagement with the argument, that the argument is simply not worth engaging with. I begin by calling this argument 'infantile'. I then spend the next three pages not really saying why, until on page 83 I finally say something about Kant having disproved the argument by questioning whether existence is more perfect than non-existence. I then continue with a few more pages of mockery, before ending on page 85 with a hilarious half-dozen comical proofs for the existence of God that I found on the Internet.

86 - 87 **The argument from beauty.** I quote a composer who asked the question, "If you have Mozart to listen to, why would you need God?" Well, the obvious answer is to create Mozart, but I don't say this.

I say that it is not self-evident why the existence of great art might be linked with the existence of the enemy. Remember that to one of our people, nothing about the enemy is going to be self-evident. *We know* that great art suggests the transcendent. Many composers have said themselves that they believe they are not alone in creating their masterpieces and that there is 'something else' that is helping them. This is very common amongst highly creative people – however most people have not experienced this and so, nicely for us, simply write it off as arty types just being a bit odd.

87 - 92 **The argument from personal 'experience'.** This is a tricky one because one of the main reasons that most of the enemy's people believe he exists is because they are convinced that they have had some

kind of experience of him (which, in most cases, they probably have). The way I attack this is by pointing out that there are a lot of people who believe they have had supernatural experiences who are obviously deluded. This is something that most believers worry about from time to time anyway, so we have that working in our favour.

I am doing several things here. I am using the 'proof by example' fallacy to suggest that just because some people have delusional spiritual experiences, this means that all spiritual experiences must be delusional.

I mention the Yorkshire Ripper's claim that Jesus told him to kill women. I do not mention what the enemy's book says about this sort of thing; that humans should expect such experiences and that they should 'test the spirits' (I think that is how he put it – it is not a book I make a habit of reading regularly) to see whether they are from him.[7]

I am also not for one moment allowing the suggestion that it may be atheists themselves who are the deluded ones (although that tiresome *Book* says this). Atheism is simply presented as the default belief given the lack of any 'evidence' (remember my definition of evidence) for anything supernatural. Atheism conveniently, by being the default, is exempt from requiring evidence. In fact a lack of any evidence is all the evidence you actually need. As they say, 'No evidence is good evidence.'

I mention the complexity of the brain, and its ability to deceive itself at times. The implication is that naturally anything that may suggest an experience of the enemy is probably something else.

I end by saying that personal experiences are not likely to be very convincing to anybody else. In a sense I could be accused of missing the point. Some people would say that the very essence of a personal experience is that it is personal. I do not mention the fact that other people's personal experiences do become very convincing to people who have had similar experiences. My scribe is safe here, as he has never had, as far as I know, any such experience. It wouldn't matter anyway now; his armour has grown extremely strong over the years.

92 - 97 **The argument from scripture.** I couldn't resist a swipe at an old enemy here. How I hated C. S. Lewis. To imagine that fifty years ago I would have got away with suggesting that he was the sort of person not used to asking questions about literature. It amused me greatly to write this!

In this section I take advantage of most people's incredible lack of biblical knowledge to suggest very strongly that the enemy's *Book* is not in any sense reliable. Most of the things I use as evidence could be countered very easily by any half-competent scholar, but what is the likelihood that the reader is going to be one of those! It is almost as improbable as the enemy existing – but not quite, obviously. Good advice would be to make the most of the nineteenth century scholars. Most of them were on our side anyway.

97 - 103 **The argument from admired religious scientists.** When I first found this quote from Bertrand Russell saying that "the immense majority of intellectually eminent men disbelieve in the Christian religion" I thought for a moment that he was quoting the enemy's *Book*, which we know says that we should expect this to be the case![8] Something about the

125

enemy preferring to use fools – no, I don't get it either. It is, thankfully, just human nature for Christians to want big names to be on their side. This is because they really want to persuade non-believers that Christianity is true and they think that big names on their side will help them to do this. This displays a fundamental misunderstanding of how the enemy works, held even by many of his own people. That 'Apostle' Paul (don't worry - we remember the *real* Saul) tried hard to do away with this, but was largely unsuccessful.[9] This is great for us, because we can exploit it by trying to imply that because not many great scientists are Christians, this means that Christianity is not a plausible worldview. This fallacy works because spectators are hardly ever aware of the amount of invisible compromise that is at work, and neither should they be. That's why it's called *invisible*.

103 - 105   **Pascal's Wager.** This one is very easy simply to ridicule, but I add a few little enhancements to spice things up a little. These enhancements are, need I say it, false.

I claim that believing in something is not something I can do as an act of the will. This is, although I do not say it, a deliberate dig at Pascal, who knew that things were really far more complicated than that (remember how Einstein said that things should always be made as simple as possible, but not simpler). Pascal himself said, "People almost invariably arrive at their beliefs not on the basis of proof but on the basis of what they find attractive."[10] What Pascal knew about that many of my readers hopefully will not is this idea of invisible compromise again. Hopefully my readers will believe that they can be objective on these kinds of issues. If this is the case then the trick will work.

I then use some false dichotomies along with the Kellogg's Cornflakes Suggestion in order to create something quite deceptive.

I ask what is so special about believing. I say that you have these various different options; you can believe, or you can be kind, or you can be generous and so on, and I ask the question *what is the one thing you must do?*, using the Kellogg's Cornflakes Suggestion perfectly, so that while we are thinking *what is the one thing?*, we have let the presupposition 'that there is only one thing' slip by unnoticed. This is a dichotomy with six options; belief, kindness, generosity, humility, sincerity, and honest truth-seeking. It is, however, a false dichotomy and again, I use the Kellogg's Cornflakes Suggestion. *But why, in any case, do we so readily accept the idea that the one thing you must do if you want to please God is believe in him?* In the process of considering why we readily accept the idea, we fail to notice that the idea 'that we should and do readily accept the idea' is false. The enemy's *Book* again does makes this clear, but what do people know about that nowadays?

I then give another false dichotomy mixed with the Kellogg's Cornflakes Suggestion when I ask whether God would prefer faked belief or honest scepticism. Hopefully nobody will consider whether there is such a thing as an honest belief.

105 - 107   **Bayesian arguments.** This section builds on my straw man god idea. It's really one big Kellogg's Cornflake Suggestion. By attempting to work out statistically how probable the enemy's existence is, people will automatically not question that such a thing can be worked out, and that such a procedure can be applied to the enemy.

107   I give an example on this page of a religious scientist who admits that there is no evidence for the enemy and seems to agree with *my* definition of 'faith'. However, I don't say who this scientist is! I put that in really as a bit of a joke aimed at those Christians who have been saying that no Christian uses the word 'faith' in the way that I do.

108   I say that religious people can't tell the difference between what is true and what they want to be true. What I am always doing when I say this sort of thing is trying to imply that if you want something to be true, then that makes it less likely to actually be true. In fact, *we know* it doesn't imply anything of the sort. Whether we want something to be true or not bears no relation to whether it is actually true or not. I don't suggest that the same idea could be applied to the atheist's position, because, as we also know, that just *is* true, and the atheist does not want, or not want, that to be true (because they are objective) and anyway, they don't go in for all of that 'faith' nonsense (which I've redefined, remember). Hopefully you can see how all of my little arguments are starting to come together nicely. Glorious!

       I even get the chance to call the enemy 'nasty' again before finishing the chapter, just in case anybody had forgotten about this.

Why There Almost Certainly is no God

113   **The ultimate Boeing 747.** What can I say? More misrepresentation. More straw men. If a method seems to be working, why change it? I say that the 'argument from design' claims that for the universe to be the way it is without a designer would be extremely improbable. I then say that the truth is

128

actually the opposite; that the argument from improbability comes close to proving that the enemy does *not* exist. At this point I have already made my first deceptive move. I emphasise the word *not* in order to suggest that theists are using the argument from improbability to prove that the enemy *does* exist. We know that this is actually not what they do. What they say is that (as I have said) for the universe to be the way it is without a designer would be extremely improbable. The statement they make is *about the universe*. They are not saying that therefore the existence of the enemy is therefore highly probable. What they are saying is that, in their opinion, the view that he created the universe, and that is why it is the way it is, is the one that makes the most sense. They do not talk about the 'probability of God existing'. That is what *we* do. The difference is only subtle, but very important, which is why we should make the most of it whenever we can.

The next thing I do is attempt to make Christians look ignorant – not a difficult thing to do. We know that no serious creationist, for example, thinks that evolutionists believe that a horse suddenly appeared one day fully formed by chance, and most of them *do* understand what is meant by natural selection. However, if I can make people believe that they don't, then the reader will possibly suspect that he or she doesn't either, and I can then make my spurious claim. I say that natural selection is not about chance. This is obviously nonsense, but I play the same game with the word 'chance' as I play with the word 'faith'. Let me explain. From the enemy's point of view, extremes are rarely good. This is the way he has created people. Too much food is bad; not enough food is bad. Too much money is bad (they have illusions of independence from him); too little money is bad (they may be tempted to steal) and

so on.[11] Humans were designed to be happy with
moderation. From our point of view, extremes are
good. Therefore we also use words in extreme ways
and always make out that there is nothing in between.
Hence the only kind of 'faith' that I talk about is
sheer blind faith; the sort of faith that has *no evidence*
to back it up (I'm sure you've heard me speak of this
before). The opposite of this is insisting on empirical
proof for everything before believing it. Both of
these are good as far as we are concerned. (Real
faith, as we know, is based on evidence. It goes one
step further than the evidence can take you, but it is
only a step and not a leap, and it is in the direction of
the evidence and not in the face of it.) I do a similar
thing with the word 'chance'. Natural selection is
either by chance or it isn't. I claim that Christians
believe that something like a horse could arrive fully
formed by chance. That is the extreme I use to
misrepresent them. I say, on the contrary, that natural
selection is not a theory of chance. In fact I say it is
the opposite. Now obviously this would not work if
there were not some truth in it. As you know, the
way natural selection works is that the creatures best
able to survive will be the ones with the best
opportunity to pass on their genes. The way that the
strongest survive is by fighting it out, and this is not
really a process of chance any more than the outcome
of a football match is a process of chance. There may
be chance elements involved but, overall, it is down
to something else. Evolution however, when we are
discussing how, let's use the same example as before,
a horse could come into existence is a process that
must involve large elements of chance, as it would
have to take millions of little steps, each containing a
little bit of chance. Also people tend to forget (if I
can successfully make them) that natural selection is
a bit like reason. Just as you can only apply reason to
presuppositions or sense experiences in order to

discover new truths (something else I like people to forget), natural selection can only create new forms of life when you already have life to begin with. How these non-living atoms arranged themselves into the suitable molecules needed for life must have been a matter of pure chance. Obviously, how non-living matter became living is still a complete mystery as far as science is concerned. They have never seen it happen (and as we know, probably never will). With every generation of organism (by the way, nobody asks how these creatures first developed the ability to reproduce – well, that must have been by chance surely?), the random mutations that occur happen by chance. The way the 'beneficial' mutations are selected may not be by pure chance but this is really the only part that is not by chance (which is why it is the only part we focus on). The correct mutations must come along at just the right time, which is again a matter of chance. Do you see what I mean? I am right that most of my opponents do not know enough about evolution to successfully debate my scribe on the issue, but why should they? Many of them don't believe in it! Do you see my scribe debating people on theology? Of course not. He doesn't believe in that, so we use more reliable methods such as ridicule. As a result, when my scribe says to a creationist that natural selection is not a process of chance, they very rarely know what to say in response. I am careful to make sure that he does not debate the ones that do, although the reasons we give as to why he does not debate them may not accurately reflect my motives as laid out here.

114   Here I say that Darwinian natural selection is the 'only known solution' to where the information in our genes comes from. It amazes me that I can get away with saying things like this. The word 'known' is interesting. It sounds so certain, don't you think?

Obviously what I mean is that it is the only possible theory that we have yet come up with (not that we are searching for others – this one will do just fine for now). But, wait a minute, what if some people ask why 'God created the world and us with it' is not another known solution? What do we say to that? Well, obviously it is 'not scientific' (remember our presupposed materialism). Never mind whether it is true or not! If they press you, try saying it's 'just too easy'!

Now I come to the crux of my argument which is basically the following. If I try to explain the existence of a statistically improbable entity, such as a horse, by invoking a designer, then the designer himself has got to be at least as improbable. Therefore the enemy is the ultimate Boeing 747, as he must be the most improbable entity of all. This argument is really great. Utterly wrong, but great. Do you see what is going on here? The two options in question are the Christian creationist-type one which states that creatures were designed by an eternal uncreated God, or the atheist evolutionary one (for want of a better name) which states that all creatures evolved by natural selection from lifeless matter. What I basically say is that if you invoke a creator (in other words, you adopt the Christian position), then your God almost certainly does not exist because he will be very improbable due to his complexity. This conclusion, however, belongs to the atheist's evolutionary position, not the Christian's! To put it another way, what I am saying is that if you suppose God created horses and that creationism is true and evolution is false, then God couldn't have created horses because, according to evolution, God even existing would be so improbable because he is so complex. The problem obviously is that if we suppose that creationism is true and evolution is false, you cannot then argue against creationism with evolution because we have just supposed it to be false! We do, however, do this and we usually get away with it.

What I do next is split the horns of a dilemma, or expose a false dichotomy, as I see it. I say that many people think that the only two options are that 'creatures were designed' or that they 'came about by chance'. I say that Darwinian natural selection is a third option that is neither design nor chance. This obviously deliberately misses the point. We know that life beginning in the first place, before natural selection could start to work, must have been a product of chance. I do not really concern myself with where the original life came from however, because then I would have to admit that there was an element of chance involved in my position. One historical way of avoiding this problem of chance has been to say that the enemy created the initial forms of life and then natural selection did the rest. Although this idea is sometimes used by us, it is obviously no good to us here as, in this book, we are arguing that the enemy does not exist and never has existed.

I tell people to be wary of assuming that design is the only alternative to chance and that just because life appears to be improbable, we don't have to jump to the conclusion that it was designed just because we can't imagine any alternative. But why would they want to imagine an alternative? If it appears to be designed, why are they not happy to conclude that it probably was? This brings me to another important point. Never forget the main reason for all of this. Humans are all rebels at heart. They are on our side really. They don't *want* to believe in him, no matter how obvious his existence is. Also, don't be as naïve as to think that any of this really matters. The 'argument from design' is hardly ever the reason why these people believe in the enemy. Most of them claim to have *met* him. Arguments like this are only ever really used in an attempt to try to convert *our* people. As somebody once said, "What presumptuous optimism!"

116 **Natural Selection as a consciousness-raiser.** What we must do is get rid of the enemy completely, and here is how we do this. In the past we have been able to accuse Christians (due to a common misunderstanding of how he works that we have been able to take advantage of) of adopting a 'god of the gaps' philosophy. By this I mean that Christians will invoke the enemy directly whenever a naturalistic explanation is not available for something. Gradually, over the years, the advance of science has been able to eliminate the enemy from many areas where his presence was once thought to be required. The problem that remains for us is that there are some things that there is still no materialistic explanation for. So what do we do? The answer is that we create our own god of the gaps. You may have heard of it – it's called 'natural selection'. Now, not even the most stubborn creationist will deny that natural selection is a fact of life. What they do deny is that there is any evidence to show that one species can change into another completely different species by means of these small adaptations that natural selection selects. In other words, they would say that lots of little changes do not necessarily add up to the big changes. In other words, according to a creationist, natural selection can do certain things, but there are also many things that it cannot do. What I say on this page of the book is that natural selection explains *the whole of life* and a full understanding of it allows us *to move boldly into other fields*, such as theology, which of course doesn't exist.

Now here I am being deliberately ambiguous. What do I mean by *the whole of life*? Do I mean the whole of biology? Or do I mean everything that there is to know about anything? I want this to be a little bit ambiguous for the reader. I am going to use my claim that a full understanding of natural selection allows us to move boldly into other fields quite a lot, and of course what I really do mean is that I am going to attempt to explain everything there is to know about anything using natural selection. I think this is sometimes called 'universal Darwinism'. Now, without a shadow of a doubt, for my scribe to hold this view, which he does, is an act of faith. It is also an act of faith by *our definition* (in other words against the evidence, even in the teeth of the evidence). It doesn't matter that in other parts of the book I claim that atheists do not have faith. Contradictions are allowed as long as nobody notices them. Obviously natural selection *does not* explain the whole of life. To begin with, natural selection does not explain the *meaning* of anything. This doesn't matter. I just dismiss all questions of meaning as being meaningless. Questions of meaning aside, it does not explain the origin of life, it does not explain the nature of human consciousness; it does not even explain the appearance of new forms of life, since this is caused by mutation; natural selection only explains how some organisms survive and some do not. One of our own scientists, who was something of a renegade (Stephen Jay Gould) wrote a rather embarrassing essay on this subject, called *Darwinian Fundamentalism*, in which he called my scribe a 'Darwinian fundamentalist' and said that his views were actually a *caricature* of natural selection.[12] Well, *of course they are a caricature!* This is the whole point! Doesn't he realise that magicians are never meant to explain a trick to a layperson? (Of course, Gould didn't know that *I* existed!) Here are a few other things Gould says in his essay. He points out that Charles Darwin himself said, "I am convinced that natural selection has been the main but not the exclusive means of modification." He says that "natural selection does not explain why many evolutionary transitions from one nucleotide to another are neutral, and therefore nonadaptive. Natural selection does not explain why a meteor crashed into the earth 65 million years ago, setting in motion the extinction of half the world's species." He calls my scribe's claim a "simplistic and uncompromising doctrine." He says that "the invigoration of modern evolutionary biology with exciting nonselectionist and nonadaptationist data from the three central disciplines of population genetics, developmental biology, and palaeontology makes our premillennial decade an especially unpropitious time for Darwinian fundamentalism." He also says this, which is probably the worst thing for us if anybody ever reads it: "There is something immensely beguiling about strict adaptationism – the dream of an underpinning simplicity for an enormously complex and various world." This is something that I have not mentioned so far but now seems to be a good time to do so. I present natural selection in the, let's face it, unrealistic way that I do for a very good reason. As I present it, the explanation it gives of life is very simple and has a certain elegance about it. In fact, it is rather like the Christian worldview in its simplicity and elegance, *and this is exactly the point.* If the sort of person who likes to have a neat and simple explanation is going to give up their Christian worldview and adopt another, the trick stands the best chance of working if I present them with *another neat and simple explanation.* Much of the persuasive power of my theory lies in its simplicity and apparent elegance.

The last thing we need is somebody like Gould, who is meant to be on our side, to come along and mess it all up.

117   Confirmation of the allure that a simple explanation possesses can be found in the quote from Douglas Adams, which directly follows my claim about natural selection. Adams says, "It was a concept of such stunning simplicity, but it gave rise, naturally, to all of the infinite and baffling complexity of life."[13] I think that says it all. He goes on to compare the awe inspired by natural selection with the awe that people talk about in respect of religious experience (which he called 'silly', but nevertheless he still associated the two things in his mind). The fact that he had never experienced the enemy didn't seem to bother him. He was a true convert. It's a shame he's gone.

119   **Irreducible complexity.** As I define it on page 123, a biological system is said to be 'irreducibly complex' if the removal of one of its parts causes the whole to cease functioning. The term 'irreducible complexity' was coined by Professor of Biochemistry at Lehigh University, Michael Behe, in his 1996 book *Darwin's Black Box*. He claims that there are many such systems that can be observed in nature and that their existence disproves Darwin's theory that all life evolved as the result of a step by step process of natural selection.

I begin on page 119 not by talking about irreducible complexity, but about natural selection. I quote the Jehovah's Witnesses (I can't remember why – it seems like an odd thing to have done now...) who quote David Attenborough describing a 'sponge skeleton' as *complex*. They then say that *chance* could not be the *designer* of a 'complex sponge skeleton'. I do not bother to pick up on the fact that the word 'designed' is used in a strange way here, as design is not a process of chance; it is in fact the opposite of chance. I don't mention this as I also want to use the word 'design' in unusual ways myself at times. I don't want my reader to start thinking about this word. I also do not pick up on the fact that 'chance' can never create anything, because it is not a thing in itself. Chance is merely the word we use to describe the results of seemingly random processes that we do not understand. For example, you might be looking at the clouds when you notice that one of them looks like a dog. You might say that, because nobody formed those clouds deliberately to look like a dog, that this happened by chance. However, chance is not the thing that formed the clouds into a dog-like shape. Processes at work in the atmosphere formed the clouds into the shape of a dog. By saying that the dog shape occurred by chance, I simply mean that *it was not designed by someone*. Anyway, I do not discuss the word 'chance' as the idea that I want the reader to have of the word is the one that they will doubtless have already.

David Attenborough described the skeleton as *complex*. I describe it as *improbable*. This is vital. I say that the options for creating such an improbable thing as the 'complex sponge skeleton' are not design and chance, but design and natural selection. Now, the reader will probably not notice what I have done here, but there are so many fuzzy words being used (creating, improbable, design, chance) that this is not surprising. I have actually given a blatantly circular argument. A *complex* structure is only *improbable* if you assume that it was 'created' by natural selection (according to natural selection, the more complex something is, the more improbable it is of being created because it has to go through more small steps, each of which comes about by chance). If a complex

138

structure was designed, it is not necessarily improbable at all. As a designer, I could design a complex product and then make it. How was that product improbable? It wasn't. My use of 'improbability' presupposes natural selection.

120   Here I use my straw man god to say that Intelligent Design (by which I mean that an organism was designed by the enemy) cannot be the solution to this problem of improbability (remember if it *were* designed it would not necessarily be improbable so I am using this word in a deliberately circular way) because the enemy would have to be even more improbable (remember that my straw man god 'comes into existence', not like the real God) and would therefore require an explanation of his own. This is one trick that can be used to get rid of the enemy.

121   On this page I falsely assert that creationists argue like this. The only things that could bring about a 'natural phenomenon' are design and chance. Because chance could not have brought about the phenomenon, it must have been designed.

The reason this is false is that it suggests that the only reason creationists believe that an organism has been designed is that they cannot accept the only alternative solution. It does not suggest that creationists believe a thing was designed because *there is positive evidence that it was designed.* Even I talk about 'apparent design'. Remember that in reality (if you still have any grip on that) the fact that something appears to have been designed is good evidence in favour of that thing having actually been designed. Truth doesn't always have to be counter-intuitive. Even we couldn't survive if that were the case. Actually the way I suggest that creationists

139

reason is actually how *we* reason. We believe in natural selection because *we cannot accept* that things may have been designed by the enemy. That is why I say on this page that natural selection is '*the only workable solution that has ever been suggested.*' 'Workable' is another interesting word, isn't it. Make of it what you will.

I keep on saying that what creationists mean when they say that an organism was created by chance is that the organism was created in one move, so to speak, by one act of 'chance', although chance cannot act at all as it is not a thing. Many creationists obviously do understand perfectly well what I mean when I talk about natural selection. By insisting that they do not, it gives me more and more opportunities to give more and more illustrations in order to 'clarify' the issue.

122   I say that creationists '*always* assume that biological adaptation is a question of the jackpot or nothing.' In other words, I suggest again that creationists always say that an organism must appear fully formed or it will not appear at all. This is obviously not true. Again I exploit my reader's ignorance. We know that creationists do not always assume this at all. I then say that creationists say that either an eye sees or it doesn't, and that there are no useful intermediates. I reply (to my own 'straw statement') by saying that this is 'simply wrong' and that these intermediates abound in practice – not that I actually give any examples! My language, as you may have noticed, is deceptively circular here. My use of the word 'intermediates' presupposes evolution by natural selection. What we actually see 'in practice' are *various different kinds of eyes*, some 'better' than others. It is only our evolutionary interpretation that makes them 'intermediates'. All we are actually

seeing are various types of eyes. A creationist explanation would just be that the enemy made various different kinds of eyes, designed for different purposes. Of course, I don't mention this.

123   I say that Darwin 'effortlessly' explained how the eye evolved by gradual stages of natural selection. This is, of course, a ridiculous claim but I like to see how far I can go and still get away with it. He gave *his opinion* of how it *could have* happened. In other words, he made up a story; and this is, amazingly, all you have to do to beat irreducible complexity. Just come up with any possible explanation that involves any hypothetical structures that you like and this will automatically be regarded as 'the best explanation' of how whatever it is came about. It will always beat the infinitely improbable 'God hypothesis'. Even if you can't come up with an explanation, simply say (as many reviewers of Michael Behe's pathetic book said) that just because we can't think of a way that something may have evolved, that does not mean it didn't evolve. If anything, it just demonstrates Behe's 'lack of imagination'! Don't you just love that?

124   On this page I claim to have just shown that eyes and wings are not irreducibly complex. Nobody has ever asked me yet exactly where I did this!

125   So I wind up this section by going back to Darwin, who started this search for irreducibly complex organs. What he actually said was this.

> "If it could be demonstrated that any complex organ existed which could not possibly have been formed by numerous, successive, slight modifications, my theory would absolutely break down. But I can find no such case."

141

And nobody ever will, because all you need to be able to do to dismiss any suggested candidate for irreducible complexity is make up a good story, and our people have a lot of experience when it comes to making up stories. Besides, our people have been immunised against the idea that you can accept the enemy as the best explanation of the evidence for anything by the principle of invisible compromise. Remember that many of them are not aware of their biases and actually think that they are being objective.

125 -
127
The worship of gaps. The 'god of the gaps' is another mistake some theologians have made in the past; invoking the enemy directly whenever there is something that, at the time, cannot be explained scientifically. Although this is something that really is practiced by some religious people, I take advantage of my reader's (hopefully) ignorance and act as though virtually all religious people are guilty of this. This is a deliberately crass generalisation on my part. The truth is (by which I mean the part I don't write down) that at least since Thomas Aquinas, in the thirteenth century, most theologians have not thought about the world in this way. The way the enemy really works is by means. In other words, things can have a scientific explanation, but that doesn't alter the fact that he is behind that process. In fact, as we know, the enemy claims that it is only by his sustaining power that we even continue to exist. Personally, I must say that I have not been shown enough evidence to believe this.

128-
134
I lie on page 128 about creationists. Most people know little enough about these people that you can say anything you like about them and, as long as what you say is negative, it will be believed. I say that they always fill gaps with the enemy. We know

this is not true. Creationists are not generally guilty of this at all. They believe that the enemy directly created the world and everything in it at the outset, but apart from that they agree pretty much with Aquinas. Intelligent Designers are slightly different as they compromise on the evolution question and actually seem to believe in it, I think. However, it is in our favour if we lump them all together and ignore their differences. And anyway, who cares who is guilty of 'the god of the gaps'? This is Christianity. Isn't everybody meant to be guilty?

135 - 141 **The anthropic principle: planetary version.** Here I defend our weak point; the origin of life. I use quite an odd and difficult to follow argument; but then I'd have to, wouldn't I? I say that for life to arise from non-life could be a very improbable event, then I say that it would not surprise me if, in the next few years, chemists create life in the laboratory. (I do not mention that if they do, it will be the result of *intelligence* – hopefully we still require that of our chemists!) I go on to say that although the probability of life arising from non-life is exceedingly low, it could happen, because it has already happened once. Now it should be obvious that, given the trillions of planets in the universe, if life *could* arise spontaneously from non-life then it probably would and yes, we would have to be just one of those lucky planets. This is the old 'it is extremely improbable that you will win the lottery but somebody wins it every week' argument. The problem is that, for all we know, it could be *impossible* for life to arise from non-life by natural processes. If that were the case, then it doesn't matter how many planets you have, it doesn't make any difference, you will not get life *anywhere*. This is what most Christians believe and when we say that it has happened once, we are of course using a

circular argument, *assuming* that life on earth came about by natural processes. We actually have *no evidence* for this belief. Unfortunately, if I'm being honest, it is *faith*, in exactly the same way that the Christian belief that life was created by God is faith.

141 – 143	**The anthropic principle: cosmological version.** I describe how improbable it is that our universe should be so finely tuned that it is able to support life. I then dismiss the solution that the enemy tuned it this way by saying that he is even more improbable than the universe. Hopefully, people have accepted my 'improbable God' argument previously and will therefore accept it again here.
144 - 147	I then give the most commonly believed alternative to a designer God tuning the universe for life. This is the 'multiverse'. This idea says that there are countless universes, all tuned slightly differently, and out of all these there must be one capable of supporting life. Obviously it must be ours because otherwise we wouldn't be here. This is another example of the 'all you have to do is make up a story' idea. Any idea at all, even an infinite number of universes, is more likely than the enemy, because we have already established that our straw man god is *the most improbable* being imaginable. You can't lose.
147 – 151	Next I bring on a poor stooge. I do pity them, being used in this way, but it's their own fault. Poor old Richard Swinburne. He gives some 'god of the gaps' type illustration to do with electrons (which I don't pick up on because it's not in my interests to do so here) and it really is a joy to behold. If only he had taken heed of the enemy's warning not to answer a fool according to his folly, or you will indeed become like him yourself."[14] He falls straight into our trap.

151 -   **The interlude at Cambridge.** Time for insulting
156   people again. This time it is scientists involved with
         the Templeton Foundation. I basically say that the
         money offered by the foundation corrupts scientists
         who would usually have nothing to do with religion,
         and makes them pretend to be religious. I'm
         surprised I can get away with this.

         On page 155 when I describe the enemy as not being
         an explanation, be sure to note that I have redefined
         'explanation' to mean 'naturalistic explanation'. Of
         course the enemy is an explanation technically. It's
         just not one that we like.

157 -   I end by restating my objections to the argument from
159   design. Now, before you start to think I am ignorant,
         I know that the argument from design is *not* the
         reason why people generally become Christians. The
         reason people get converted is because they believe
         they have had some kind of experience of the enemy.
         On top of that they believe that the *Book* (in spite of
         what we say about it) is uncannily accurate about
         how it describes them, and is remarkably internally
         consistent (although we will deny this whenever we
         can as not many people read it anymore so how will
         they know any different?) Anyway, we must do all
         that we can.

The Roots of Religion

163 -   **The Darwinian imperative.** Do you remember my
166   'all you have to do is make up a story' idea from the
         last chapter? This is what this chapter is all about.
         It's all a story. I start by saying that we know we are
         products of Darwinian evolution (which some of my
         readers will agree with), and start to speculate about
         the origins of religion from this. Note that this is all

one big circular argument. I am absolutely presupposing atheism here right from the outset.

166 -
169
Direct advantages of religion. I continue speculating here and hopefully do this in such a way that masks my lack of any evidence for all of this.

169 -
172
Group selection. More of the same. As my scribe's arch-nemesis says, bludgeon the reader into submission through the power of your assertions, or something like that.

172 -
179
Religion as a by-product of something else. Here I suggest that religion could have been some sort of evolutionary mistake. I also manage to quote a bit of Tennyson along the way. I even get to indulge in a bit more mockery at the end.

179 -
180
Psychologically primed for religion. I rather like something that I say at the bottom of page 179, going over to 180 (again, I almost can't believe I actually said this – I know it can't be doing me any favours, but I couldn't resist it). I said that a dualist is anybody who believes that we have a soul (so basically most religious people) and that we are not just matter – okay so far. Anyway, what I then say is that dualists (so all religious people) believe that most mental illnesses are a result of 'demon possession' (as if *they* exist!), and that they will at any opportunity personify clouds and waterfalls, seeing spirits and demons in them. Now, I know this might make me sound very ignorant (of course, we know that I don't really believe these things), but... I don't know, maybe I'll regret saying things like this one day. Probably not.

181 -
191
The rest of this section is just wild speculation with bits of insult and mockery interspersed, except for a

bit at the end about Luther. I include some quotes from Martin Luther (who would, of course, probably have been an atheist if he'd lived today) seeming to say that reason is the enemy of faith. In fact he does say this. He says, "Reason is the greatest enemy that faith has" and "Reason should be destroyed in all Christians." This is interesting because it really does show what powerful effects can be achieved simply by accurately quoting people (you can find all sorts of things like this on the Internet, you know). As my scribe's current arch-nemesis puts it in his book,

> "No attempt is made to clarify what Luther means by 'reason', and how it differs from what Dawkins takes to be the self-evident meaning of the word. What Luther was actually pointing out was that human reason could never fully take in a central theme of the Christian faith – that God should give humanity the wonderful gift of salvation without demanding they do something for him first."[15]

He goes on to describe my engagement with Luther as 'inept'! Inept indeed! Doesn't anybody appreciate a good magic trick these days?

191 - 201 **Tread softly, because you tread on my memes.** This is my scribe's idea of a hypothetical replicator for ideas, called a 'meme', similar to a gene, except that genes are real and we have evidence for them, but for the moment, let's just forget about evidence, or let's just redefine it or something. No, let's just forget about it. More speculation. My scribe's idea is that religion is a virus of the mind. Obviously, atheism isn't one. Atheism is the default, obviously – don't ask me why, it just is. Have a little faith!

202 - 207 **Cargo cults.** Here I speculate about the origins of Christianity by describing how cults can spring up

very easily, and how people will attribute supernatural explanations to natural events. We know that there are a lot of false religions that exist in the form of cults, and at some point in time it probably crosses the mind of every Christian that their religion might be just another of these. We rely on the fact that there will be plenty of readers who have not given this sufficient thought.

The Roots of Morality: Why are we Good?

211 - Before I begin let me point out one thing. In a
214 previous book, my scribe has said that the universe consists has "no design, no purpose, no evil and no good, nothing but blind pitiless indifference."[16] Now, I think he still maintains this view but for this chapter of *this* book however, we must assume that at least 'good' does exist, otherwise none of it will make any sense. So, if you will excuse this apparent inconsistency (don't worry - it is only apparent), I will continue.

I start this chapter by bringing on several stooges. They are all 'religious' people. I give these examples because I want to show the reader that many religious people say evil things, as if they didn't know this already. So why do we need religion in order to be good?

214 - **Does our moral sense have a Darwinian origin?**
222 Here I give a Darwinist's explanation of why people are good. Obviously, like everything else, it is so they can propagate their 'selfish genes', but there is a problem…

221 There are a few situations that don't quite fit. I give the examples of adopting somebody else's child and

showing mercy to a debtor as our Darwinian instincts 'misfiring'. So that nobody thinks I am saying that these actions are bad, I describe them as blessed, precious mistakes. What I mean is that sometimes we can be 'good' even when we are being 'un-Darwinian', as I put it. Whether the reader realises it or not, at this point I have a big problem. Nowhere do I ever define what I mean by 'good'. This is not an accidental oversight on my part. I don't define it, because *everybody knows* what 'good' means and I just act as though this is quite normal. What the reader hopefully will not realise is that this idea that we all have a built-in knowledge of what 'good' means is a part of the enemy's worldview, not ours. Hopefully this theft will go unnoticed, and unpunished.

222 -
226

A case study in the roots of morality. Here I give various scenarios involving moral decisions in order to show that atheists and religious people generally make the same moral choices. My conclusion is that we therefore do not need the enemy in order to be good or evil. My argument is that we have all evolved the same moral intuition, so therefore we are all the same in this respect. Obviously, this is a sort of red herring. We are making a point that nobody would really argue with when we say that both atheists and religious people generally make the same moral choices. The difference is in how this is explained. The enemy's people say that all humans share the same knowledge of what good and evil mean because they are all made in his image. This means that to them 'good' is a real thing, grounded in the very character of the enemy. We therefore have to define it in some other way, although our definitions never seem to be as convincing as we would like them to be. People always seem to feel cheated by them, and a good trick should never do that. It is important that you do not forget that what we are trying to do is give a pseudo-explanation of why the world is the way it is. Like any good explanation that happens not to be true, it will explain some parts of reality better than others. It can achieve a lot by being reductionist (for example, our explanation really leaves out explanations of things like consciousness, the origin of life – of course, if pushed, we can come up with something to say but we try to avoid this if at all possible – either that or call the enemy's people 'arrogant' for claiming to have answers, whereas we are humble, and humble is obviously 'good' for some reason, I can't remember why we say that is – oh, yes, it says so in the enemy's *Book*! – let's ignore that for the moment), but some aspects of life, such as our sense of good and evil, are too obvious to leave out although we haven't yet got our pseudo-explanation of them quite right.

226 **If there is no God, why be good?** When they say the devil is in the details, they don't know how close to the truth they are. This section is a lesson in equivocation which, if you remember, is the art of using the same word in two different ways in order to mislead. The word in question here is 'good'. It has two meanings that are subtly different. The first meaning of good, used by *his* people, is a standard of behaviour grounded in the very nature of the enemy. As a result, because the enemy creates humans in his own image, they have an innate knowledge of what is good and what is evil. The 'moral law' is the name given to the laws that humans are born knowing that tell them what good behaviour is. Good, in this sense, is a real standard. The other meaning of the word 'good' is when it is used to describe what a person considers to be favourable or beneficial based on some other criteria, which may vary in origin. In this sense, 'good' behaviour may be 'whatever brings

the most happiness to the most people' or 'whatever best aids the survival of the species' or any other definition you care to give it. Because the concept of 'good' is not grounded in the absolute character of the enemy, people can say things like 'one man's evil is another man's good' and other such nonsense. Sometimes this gets called moral relativism. The enemy's followers like to try to use the fact that people generally believe that good and evil are real things in order to lead them to him. If you've not heard their argument I'll tell it to you so you'll recognise it when you hear it. The idea is that if you do believe that good and evil are real things, and that what has been called the moral law is a real law, then it follows, they say, that somebody must have given that law, as laws don't just appear by themselves. This is pretty strong evidence for the enemy's existence, as well we know. It is therefore very important that we try to create as much confusion as possible with regard to these two meanings of the word 'good'.

226 –
230

Here's how it works. I start off by asking the question 'if there is no God, why be good?' This is a deliberate ploy on my part. I ask the enemy's followers if is true that the only reason they are good is because they fear punishment from the enemy. If they say that they would be good even without him, I say that therefore there is no reason to say that God is necessary in order for us to be good. Checkmate. I win. It is important for you to see that this argument wonderfully misses the whole point; however I still keep it going for several pages. Obviously, what Christians are saying is *not* that without the enemy, people would not be good. What they are saying is that without him, *there would be no such thing as good.* All there would be is behaviour I personally like or find in some way beneficial. For this reason,

151

the question I originally asked is meaningless. If I were playing fairly, I could not ask 'if there is no God, why be good?' if I mean 'good' in the real sense, because if there is no God, *there is no good to be*, so by assuming the first half of the question to be true, I have rendered the second half of the question meaningless. Of course for people to be 'good' in our sense, the enemy need not exist, but what 'good' actually then becomes is not what most readers will have in mind. This is absolutely classic equivocation. Watch and learn. They will still be thinking of what they know, which is this absolute standard that tells them, for example, when they hear of a child being kidnapped and murdered, that it is *not* a reasonable defence for the murderer to say 'one man's evil is another man's good.' Evil really exists, and good really exists. We know it is not just a matter of our own opinion.

There is something else also at work here that I will mention. Hopefully, by now, I have repeated the fact that the God of the Bible is a tyrant and a bully enough times for it to be taken for granted, at least subconsciously, by most of my readers. What I try to make people overlook when I talk about Christians only being good because they fear punishment from God, is that I am being a reductionist here *and* using a caricature. We do not have this with our father below, but the enemy actually enters into a relationship with his followers. He *really is* their father and the question of obedience should only really be considered in this context. If we were to ask a human child if the only reason they were ever good was because they feared punishment from their human father, they would of course say no – obedience is a response to that thing they call love. If we were to ask them if fear of their human father *ever* meant that they behaved in a way that was good when

152

otherwise they might have been bad, then they would probably say that sometimes it did. They would probably also say, particularly if asked years later, that this was a 'good' thing. We forget sometimes that there is a type of fear that is beneficial to humans; the kind of fear that stops them doing dangerous things.

230   I know that not all of my readers will fall for this, so here's what I do next (only after four pages of red herrings though). I actually acknowledge the real problem. I give it as a statement from an 'imaginary apologist'. You may wonder why I do this when there are many well-known apologists (like our old enemy C. S. Lewis) that I could have quoted. Hopefully, the answer is obvious. Firstly, to some readers it may appear that *I thought of this problem myself*; but that will be very few readers indeed. No, the main reason is, of course, that if I'd given a quote from a book by C. S. Lewis, some of my readers may have gone off and *read the book I quoted from*! The consequences of that, I'm sure you can imagine, would not be 'good' (according to our definition of the word!).

231   I attempt to kill off any curiosity aroused by my discovery by immediately following it up with a confusion statement. I exchange the word 'good' for 'moral' and make some statement about the 'likelihood of God's existence' (remember to keep bringing the same ideas back again and again to reinforce them). It really is a nonsense sentence. Read it again and see what I mean. I then flounder a little and repeat myself a few times in order to really disorientate the reader. Then I start talking about Kant.

231-   This business of talking about Kant is simply to show

232　　that there have been attempts at working out definitions of 'good' that don't involve God. It is just another red herring. On the next page, I admit that Kant's arguments are not convincing. I, of course, claim Kant as an atheist (while admitting that, of course, he wasn't one – isn't that clever - but would have been if only he had lived two hundred years later). What my scribe would be if he lived two hundred years into *his* future never seems to be considered. Never let the relativisers be relativised![17]

232　　After dismissing Kant, I have hopefully given the reader enough time to forget what we are talking about. I now give another ambiguous phrase. I mention '*morals*' again, being '*driven by religion*'. Now what this means is, hopefully, anybody's guess. What I really mean is '*good' grounded in the character of God* but I am shifting the ground a little and wouldn't dare speak too openly at this point. I now confuse the matter further by citing classic 'hard cases' in morality. Hopefully, what the reader will conclude is that if we cannot answer a hard question, this means that the question has no answer, and neither does any other.

232　　Hopefully you will notice that although I began this section arguing that we could be good without the enemy, I am no longer using the word 'good' at all. Its absence will hopefully go unnoticed for the remainder of the chapter. I make a statement about morals not having to be absolute, as if that were *our* idea. We know that the enemy is well aware that in this fallen world the best that can be achieved is often the lesser of two evils. He makes provision for this many times in his *Book*. Fortunately for us though, the lesser of two evils is still evil.

232 –　I end the chapter with a collection of ideas. I agree

233   that it is hard to defend 'absolutist morals' without religion. The word 'absolutist' makes a person sound bad. Coupled with my 'hard cases' this should be enough to fool most people. I then play the problem down by describing the claim that real good cannot exist without the enemy (although I do not say those words) by calling the claim hypothetical (and it *is* hypothetical in the sense that I didn't bother to quote anybody!). I confuse the issue by mentioning patriotism, cast aspersions on the enemy's *Book* again (as a diversion) and just for good measure call religious people hypocrites (as if that were relevant). I end by saying (just to get the word in) that the fact they are hypocrites is a 'good' thing. Hopefully the reader will be so keen to begin the next chapter that they will not stop to question what I actually mean here by 'good'!

The 'Good' Book and the Changing Moral *Zeitgeist*

237   My quotation on page 235 is actually a play on something from the Old Testament.[18] I begin properly by saying that the Ten Commandments are obnoxious to civilised modern people. Obviously I am not condoning disrespect to parents, murder, adultery, theft, lying and covetousness. What I am objecting to are the first four commandments, which are about the enemy; therefore what I mean by 'civilised modern people' are, basically, atheists. Don't forget – this is what I do. I use words to mean whatever I want them to mean, whenever I want them to. Don't worry about this. Everybody does it.

I do it again on the same page a bit further down. I call the religious beliefs of Bishop John Spong 'advanced'. What I mean here by 'advanced' is, basically, atheistic. The more you do this kind of thing, the more natural it will become. Soon, you won't even realise that you're doing it.

237 -
250
The Old Testament. The order of the day here is circularity; both magic and non-magic. The non-magic, traditional, plain old circularity can be seen in the way that all my arguments assume that atheism is true and judge the enemy's *Book* in this light.

The magic circularity is made possible due to the very nature of the enemy himself. God, as we know, is said to be a loving God. He is also called a just God. Because of this, there will be many places in his *Book* that speak of his infinite love and other passages that speak of his terrible judgements. All we have to do is emphasise the judgement side without mentioning the loving side. It's easy; almost *too easy*.

250 -
253
Is the New Testament any better? I praise Jesus for breaking away from the Old Testament (do you see the way presuppositions affect the way I interpret the evidence?) but criticise him for being rude to his mother. You may be interested to know that, in a recent article, my scribe speculated that Jesus, if he were alive today, would actually be an atheist.[19] I think so too. Don't you? I then go on to mock and misinterpret the New Testament for all it's worth. I feign ignorance with regard to theology (remember, it's not a real subject) and ask questions like why couldn't the enemy just have forgiven people without killing his son? Obviously, I know the answer to this, but I don't engage with it here. It is not in our interests for me to do so.

254 –
262
Love thy neighbour. I continue in the same way. Magic circularity. Pick out bad-sounding verses. Quote them out of context. Do not, under any

circumstances, try to get to the bottom of what they really mean. Who cares what they really mean? I certainly don't.

262 -
272
The moral Zeitgeist. Here I argue that humanity is getting better at being good. This is quite easy to do. You simply pick something or someone from now, that is better than something or someone from the past. For example, Hitler, although bad, was not as bad as Caligula. It's obviously simplistic. Caligula was ruler of the entire known world and so had the power to be a lot worse, but don't worry about this sort of thing. Here's another; the enemy's *Book* took slavery for granted, whereas we wouldn't dream of having slaves (yes, I know – remember I'm lying). Don't mention that it was Christians who got slavery abolished and that a slave in biblical times was really more like what we'd call a servant today and that they were actually treated very well! Mentioning those things would be very bad. Obviously, what an atheist considers to be 'good' will be different from what a Christian considers to be good, because they are completely different realities (or delusions). This is part of the problem we can exploit. The reason the enemy gave the law was because people *do not know* what is good, thank goodness. They can't even decide what 'good' means and what they think is good is always *not good enough*. It never has been.

272
What about Hitler and Stalin? Weren't they atheists? In this section I tried to convince my reader that atheism does not lead to violence. I knew that this would be pretty impossible to do, given the evidence of the twentieth century, so one of the things I thought I might try is to argue about whether Hitler actually was an atheist.

273 –
I begin on page 273 by saying that it doesn't matter

278   whether Hitler was an atheist or not, then spend the next five pages discussing the matter, before concluding that he probably wasn't, although I don't actually know what he was.

278   I end by saying that although many people would go to war because of something they believe in, why would anybody go to war because of an absence of belief?

On the surface, this could fool some people. Here is the truth though. What you must not forget is that our people are not people who don't believe in anything at all; they are just people who don't believe in the enemy, and if they don't believe in him then they will believe in something else, because unfortunately that is just the way they are made. Whatever this something else is, it may well be something that some of them are prepared to kill for. Although Stalin and, for example Pol Pot (not Hitler – remember, he was a Christian) didn't explicitly say, "I'm an atheist and I'm going to kill all these millions of people in the name of atheism", they did kill people in the name of socialism, which is grounded in atheism. Also, being atheists *didn't stop them* from killing millions of people. This is a tricky one that we must handle carefully.

What's Wrong with Religion? Why be so Hostile?

281 -   **Fundamentalism and the subversion of science.**
282   After my caricature on the previous page, I start this chapter with a joke, saying that I do not thrive on confrontation. I hope that made you laugh. There is, however, a reason for this statement, as it covers up a little deception that comes next. It's a loose form of a fallacy called 'affirming the consequent'. I mention

that I don't take part in debates with creationists. Now, the fact that there *is* a debate at the moment between evolutionists and creationists, particularly in America, is undeniable. Concerned though, with the amount of media attention creationists are getting, my scribe now refuses to debate them. This is how he reasons. If there really were no debate going on, he would not have to bother debating creationists. Therefore, if he refuses to debate them, it will give the impression that there is no debate going on. It's a good trick. We create the effect that there is no debate going on by acting in the way that we would if there really were no debate going on. Isn't that great?

282   I use a false dichotomy here. I call belief in a holy book an axiom and not the end result of reasoning. This works because, for most Christians, belief in a holy book *is* an axiom (once they have come to trust it) in the sense that if something (that could be interpreted in more than one way – I do not mention this because I try to make out that we can be objective and that it is usually clear how evidence should be interpreted) seems to contradict their holy book, they will usually think that it is more likely that they have misinterpreted the evidence than that their holy book (which has proved itself to be correct so many times before) is wrong. Most Christians come to treat their *Book* this way because of a process of reasoning based on how reliably well it seems to have proved itself to be in the past, so the dichotomy is therefore false. In that sense their beliefs are at the same time both axioms and conclusions. Remember that at one level or another we all deal in circles.

283   My personalised definition of 'faith' is actually multi-purpose. As well as being able to use it against religious people, I can apply it to myself when I say things such as that my belief in evolution is *not* faith.

159

284 –
286
Here I tell a story about a man who chose to follow his Bible rather than believe in evolution and then talk about how he wounded his life's happiness. I also suggest that throwing out his Bible would have been an easy thing to do and that religion is ruining peoples' minds. We know that this, naturally, is only true if atheism is true. My argument has to be circular here. I know that to suggest that people would be happier and more fulfilled if they 'simply' threw out their Bibles and embraced atheism is a claim that I could never back up with any substantial evidence (in fact the evidence would be against me), but this is the sort of thing you need to say if you are trying to argue this sort of point.

286 -
288
The dark side of absolutism. Most people (even Christians) will agree with most of this. However, the relationship between Old Testament Jewish Law and Christianity is a difficult subject. I don't engage with it at all. Why should I? If I did it would only weaken my point.

289 -
291
Faith and homosexuality. Stooges this time. When you are dealing with such a complex subject as homosexuality it shouldn't be difficult to find well meaning Christians who will say outrageous things for you. Again, whatever you do, don't attempt to engage with the actual subject. Just try to make it appear as though you have.

291 -
298
Faith and the sanctity of human life. Another tricky subject. With issues like abortion you can't lose. There are so many opinions on the subject that you can choose exactly the ones you need in order to deliver the message you want. It's also an emotional issue, so people will say things without thinking it all through properly first. This is perfect for us. On

page 294, I give an example of Christians speculating about what the enemy would think. You can't get any better than this, and of course you can bring in euthanasia. This sort of stuff is easy to do. Practically self-working magic, as they say.

298 - 301   **The great Beethoven fallacy.** At the heart of this section is a false analogy that goes like this. To abort a human foetus deprives a human being of a life. Likewise, whenever humans fail to have sexual intercourse and 'waste an egg' they deprive a human being of a life. The falsehood here is obvious. The wasted egg was almost certainly never alive in the sense that the foetus was, although what I am really doing is taking advantage of a gap in our knowledge. If we wanted to argue with Christians about at what point in time the foetus could be considered alive, then this is really a matter of faith on both our parts, as we don't know the answer either, although of course we don't have faith so it must be something else.

301 - 308   **How 'moderation' in faith fosters fanaticism.** Again there is a lot of truth here in what I say. It is the shifted dichotomy working on our side again. The distinction is not Christian or non-Christian, but rather religious or non-religious. I can then attack Christians by telling the truth for a change (although, it has to be said, it is not a pleasant experience).

I always find it rather amusing that suicide bombers are considered to be martyrs. I always thought that you become a martyr when *somebody else kills you* because of your religion?

I end by discussing whether faith is good or evil. I'm not clear here whether I am discussing faith using my definition or the normally accepted one. It doesn't matter. If people are confused, that's good. They will feel inferior because they don't understand me, and will then be more inclined to assume that whatever I say must be right because I must be clever. In reality, we know that faith is only as good or as bad as whatever it is that you have faith in.

Childhood, Abuse and the Escape from Religion

309 -
312
I don't have a lot of comments to make about this chapter as, by this point in the book, I have stopped making arguments for atheism. From now on I simply assume that I have already shown it to be true. As far as Christianity goes, I continue to judge it by its abuse.

313
I have a little joke on this page. I quote a Catholic newspaper (I am basically using them as a stooge) and then complain at how they have misused the words 'forced', 'compulsory', 'ferocious', 'fanaticism' and 'bigotry'. This comes after I, throughout the whole of this book, have been using my own versions of the words 'God', 'faith', 'evidence', 'design', 'good', 'explanation', 'advanced' and 'reason'. Since my scribe claims to have spent a lot of time, while reading Alister McGrath's book *Dawkins' God*, writing the word 'teapot' in the margin[20], I thought it only fair that I give him, at least once, the opportunity to write the words 'pot' and 'kettle' in the margin of this one. Isn't that kind of me?

314
I mock Nicolas Ridley and Hugh Latimer (both Christian martyrs burned by Queen Mary) by claiming that the differences between Protestantism and Catholicism are comparable to the difference between whether you crack open a boiled egg at the

big end or at the little end. I can make apparently ignorant comments such as these because my average reader will not know any better.

315   Another straw man. Most Christians, I think it is fair to say, would agree with me that there is no such thing as a 'Christian child', at least not in any strict sense. I am really taking advantage of a grey area of theology here, where the enemy has not given us as much detail as we would like. If he had given us more, then we could have taken even greater advantage of it, but he hasn't.

317   **Physical and mental abuse.** Here I give my opinion that the damage done by bringing up a child as a Roman Catholic is possibly worse than sexually abusing them. A bit of a dodgy one this. Not sure I didn't go too far…

318 –   Here I begin to give atheist testimonies, in the same
325   way that Christians give theirs. There are plenty to choose from. I end by making the 'sexual abuse' analogy again.

325 -   **In defence of children.** Here I say that children
331   should not be brought up being taught religious ideas. Let them make up their own minds when they are old enough.   At first, this sounds sensible, but it's disastrous in reality. If only we can get well-meaning parents to behave in this way, then the children will be ours.

331   **An educational scandal.** Here I say that no scientist ever suggested that a child is a 'chemical mutation'. This is quite right. We don't suggest it, we assert it; and it's not chemical, it's biological; and it is not a mutation but rather the end result of countless separate mutations that have occurred over millions

of years. Please get it right in future!

335   On this page I use the word 'reputable' to mean 'anyone with theologically liberal or atheistic tendencies'.

340   **Consciousness-raising again.** Again I say that children should be allowed to make up their own minds about religion when they are old enough. You see, the trick here goes like this. What we suggest by this is that you bring your child up 'neutral', without giving them any of your opinions as to which religion they should follow. In reality this is not the case because remember that there is no such thing as neutrality. If you attempt to bring your child up 'neutrally', you have not succeeded in not giving them any message about religion. What you have actually succeeded in doing is giving them the message that *it doesn't matter what religion you belong to.* Statistically speaking after that (if they ever do choose a religion) since there is only one true religion, they will most likely end up in one of our camps.

340 -   **Religious education as a part of literary culture.**
344   This is just a bit of fun. I end this chapter by saying that we shouldn't get rid of the enemy's *Book* because it is good literature and helps people, among other things, to understand the subtleties of Jeeves and Wooster stories.

        I end by saying that the *Book* is part of our treasured heritage. Considering that I have spent almost the last 350 pages calling it evil, I can't remember what I was actually thinking when I wrote this. I must have been using my own definition of the word 'treasured' that means 'promoting child abuse' or something like that. Sometimes it's hard to keep track of everything.

A Much Needed Gap?

347 -   **Binker.** Another flawed analogy. Religion is
352   like having an imaginary friend.

356   **Consolation.** I exploit my reader's ignorance
         again here by asking why not many Christians
         seem to be overly enthusiastic about the prospect
         of dying, when they supposedly believe that the
         afterlife will be so good. We know the answer, of
         course. Part of it is, surely, that the process of
         death may well be unpleasant; secondly, there are
         all the people you will leave behind; thirdly, there
         is the fear of the unknown, since believers know
         in general terms what will happen to them but not
         the details. A deeper answer, however, is of
         course that we know humans were never meant to
         die. They all know this in their souls. Remember
         that death is as an unnatural thing (and no matter
         how much time and effort we put into trying to
         promote the opposite view those humans still
         know this deep down). Unfortunately we can't
         really do anything about this.

         I then ask a silly question about why religious
         people are against suicide and euthanasia. I say
         that the official answer is that killing is a sin.
         Obviously that *is* the answer. It's not just the
         official answer. I'm really just trying to wind up
         any stubborn believers who have bothered to read
         this far, and also provide the atheists with some
         pseudo-theology to have a good laugh at.

357   I complain that euthanasia is not more readily
         available and say that my scribe will have to
         move to a more enlightened place. By

'enlightened' I obviously mean 'atheistic'.

358   On this page, it could appear that I half suggest that Cardinal Basil Hume was, in fact, a secret atheist. This is, of course, not the case. As if I'd suggest something like that...

358 –
360   I spend a few pages here talking about the lack of any evidence for the idea of 'purgatory'. This will come as no surprise to our Christian readers, as they know that purgatory is not found in the enemy's *Book*. I am again attacking a straw man.

360 -
362   **Inspiration.** Life is precious. There is no doubt about that, so you'd better make the most of it while it lasts. I suggest that the atheistic worldview is both life-enhancing and free of self-delusion. Many of the enemy's people say that they used to be atheists and find that their life is now greatly enhanced by their religious beliefs. My comment about self-delusion obviously presupposes the truth of atheism, but if I were being honest (and I suppose I can be as this is almost the end of my commentary), if somebody really, really believed that the enemy didn't exist and that their life was so short and that once they were dead that was that, then why are they so hung up on all this stuff about being deluded. Why not be deluded if it makes your life better? Maximise your enjoyment, that's what I would say. The truth is that this is just what we actually do. Our beliefs enhance our lives because it makes us free of this and free of that and free of *him*, but we know it's a delusion. Nobody is free of *him*. Not even I am really free of *him*. It's a trick. In fact, it's one of the best tricks I've ever come up with.

362 - **The mother of all burkas.** I end the main body
374   of the book with a genuinely interesting metaphor
       concerning a burka, symbolising the narrow slit
       through which humans view the world. There are
       many things we do not understand. Even I can
       say that. I leave a little message for you on page
       367. I have hidden it among the text but I will
       extract it for you. It consists of nine words, on the
       sixth and seventh lines of the page.

       "Now we understand essentially how the trick is done."

6. The Greatest Trick?

The Van Dine Principle

Have you ever read a detective novel? I occasionally do and, as with many magic tricks, I find them fascinating but also I find them immensely annoying. This is because I usually can't work out how the murder was done, and every time I get to the last chapter where the detective explains everything, I generally feel as though I should have been able to work it all out for myself quite easily, but I hardly ever do. I often used to wonder why this was.

In September 1928 Willard H. Wright, writing under the name S. S. Van Dine, wrote down what he considered to be the twenty rules of detective fiction writing. The fifteenth rule concerns how the solution to the mystery is to be concealed from the reader.

> "The truth of the problem must at all times be apparent
> – provided the reader is shrewd enough to see it. By
> this I mean that if the reader, after learning the
> explanation for the crime, should reread the book, he
> would see that the solution had, in a sense, been staring
> him in the face – that all clues really pointed to the
> culprit – and that, if he had been as clever as the
> detective, he could have solved the mystery himself
> without going on to the final chapter."[1]

It seems to me like we are all inside a detective novel. Life is a mystery and we are surrounded by clues. We just have to work it all out. As you can imagine, to somebody who can never work out how the murder in a detective novel was done, this is not very encouraging. If life does have a meaning and if the ultimate questions do have solutions, then working them all out is bound to be more difficult than working out who the murderer is in a detective novel; and I can't even do that. It doesn't help that the writer of the detective story is continually feeding us false clues that lead us away from the truth by giving us facts that seem to explain some of the mystery but not all of it. It's all very frustrating.

Pseudo-Explanations

Derren Brown has written on the importance, in mental magic, of communicating an apparent method for the achievement of mind-reading, even though this method is fictitious.[2] The pseudo-explanation has become a standard part of Derren's television trickery. One particularly memorable trick had to do with two people from an advertising agency, who were asked to come up with some posters for a taxidermy business. Once they had finished their work, and Derren revealed to them that he had predicted pretty much exactly the designs they would come up with, he revealed how the trick was done. On the way to the building where the trick was filmed, the people from the agency had been unwittingly shown all the things that they had then included in their designs. Their brains had taken in all this information subconsciously, due to the fact that their attention was never directly drawn to these things themselves. When asked to come up with an advertising campaign, these useful images automatically came to the forefront of their minds and, just as Derren had planned, they drew those exact same things. It was a great explanation of a great trick. It was, of course, almost certainly not true.[3]

But it goes further than this because once we start to believe a pseudo-explanation, we soon get very used to it and it becomes a natural part of the way in which we think. In his book *Pure Effect*, Derren Brown tells a great story about the time he performed a mind reading effect for a friend.[4] He had a dice (here I use the incorrect, but less irritating, plural version of the word 'die') with a transmitter inside that informed him, by means of a vibrating pad strapped to his leg, what number was currently being shown. He asked his friend to set the dice to any number and then visualise the face. He told his friend that he would then be able to see the pattern of dots in his friend's mind simply by observing tiny movements on his face. On the fourth attempt the dice fell apart in his friend's hand, revealing the transmitter equipment inside. His friend, however, still did not suspect that Derren was cheating. He says that it made more sense to his friend to continue to believe that Derren was reading his facial movements.

What would appear to have happened is that his friend had become very accustomed to the idea that Derren was able to tell what he was thinking by observing his tiny facial movements. When an extra piece of information came along that the pseudo-explanation didn't explain (in this case the presence of the transmitter equipment), this extra information was just ignored by his friend, in much the same way as atheists ignore, or if it is forced to their attention try to explain away, little things like morality, design and spiritual experiences.

But I think it goes even further than this. People like Richard Dawkins have an awful lot invested in their views. For Richard Dawkins at this stage in his life to become a Christian would possibly mean writing off much of his life's work. He would also lose a lot of friends. Changing your fundamental view of life is not an easy thing to do. On top of all that, admitting you were wrong can be quite an embarrassing thing to have to do. In the story about the dice Derren Brown says that, to his friend, the explanation that Derren was reading his facial movements was more appealing than the "embarrassing truth." Sometimes it is much easier to stay with the pseudo-explanation than to admit to everyone that you were taken in by a lie. But how do we know for sure which explanation is the true explanation?

Thinking Traps and Escapology

The first thing you must realise, it seems to me, is that neutrality is an illusion. Science is not neutral, Richard Dawkins is not neutral, Derren Brown is not neutral and neither am I. Whatever our position is, it is biased in one way or another, and our biases can lead us into traps.

Here is an example of what I mean. In one section of *Tricks of the Mind*, called 'Thinking Traps', Derren Brown talks about our tendency to fall prey to cognitive illusions, or mental traps.[5] Personally, I think that there is one thinking trap that magicians are more susceptible to than most people. Here is a quotation from Harry Houdini about spiritualism.

> "Magicians are trained for magical work, therefore, they detect false moves more quickly than ordinary observers who might chance to witness a séance without knowledge of the subtleness of misdirection."[6]

George Bernard Shaw said that the liar's punishment is not being able to believe anyone else. Could it be that magicians, because of their profession, have a tendency to suspect that everything they see may be a possible trick of some sort? We tend to forget that our senses are usually very reliable. That is why magic is fun. If we were constantly being deceived, why would one more deception be considered entertainment?

So let's say we think we have some kind of spiritual experience. Why should we automatically assume that we have been deceived? Why should we not take the experience at face value? It seems to me that the answer lies, yet again, in our presuppositions because to some degree they will determine our biases. If we believe in God, and believe that he can and sometimes does communicate with us, then why be cynical when we really, really, feel that he *has* communicated with us. Now, as a Christian, I would obviously add various caveats to that. The Christian worldview tells us that God is not the only spiritual being who may want to communicate with us, so we must (as the Bible puts it) test the spirits.[7] The Bible does not ask us to be gullible and believe everything a spirit may seem to be communicating to us any more than we would believe everything a magician told us on a DVD commentary, for example. There may be many people in the world who are performing counterfeit miracles, but does that mean that real miracles don't exist? If, on the other hand, you don't believe in God then, naturally, any number of 'supposed miracles' aren't going to convince you that anything supernatural is actually happening, as anything can be written off as a trick. This is a massive stumbling block for atheists. It is important to see that they come to the evidence as atheists or, as philosophers of science put it 'observation statements presuppose theory.'[8] They do not come to the evidence impartially; and if they come to the evidence as atheists, then they will almost always leave it as atheists, because almost any evidence can be simply interpreted according to their existing atheistic framework.

The only way of breaking out of this thinking trap is for the atheist first to actually *want* to break out. If they can be tempted to 'try on' another worldview and see how the evidence looks through somebody else's eyes then they may have a chance of escaping. However, if the atheist is not prepared to do this because they find their own worldview perfectly adequate, they could well be caught in a trap from which not even Harry Houdini would have been able to escape. But listen to what the Apostle Paul writes in his letter to the church in Rome.

> "Since the creation of the world God's invisible qualities – his eternal power and divine nature – have been clearly seen, being understood from what has been made, so that men are without excuse."[9]

If there really is so much evidence in the world for God that everybody is without excuse, how do atheists manage to ignore it all so easily?

Hidden in Plain View

In *Tricks of the Mind*, Derren Brown says that a common finale for stage hypnotists is to make themselves invisible. He says that "this is often termed a 'negative hallucination', where the subject is instructed *not* to see something that *is* there, instead of vice versa."[10]

Some of the earliest detective stories were written by Edgar Allan Poe. It is in his story *The Purloined Letter* that we first come across the idea of something being 'hidden in plain view'. A letter is concealed in a place where nobody will look for it; in plain view, in a vase, on the mantelpiece. It is there for everybody to see, but nobody does see it. Poe's detective, Dupin, explains it like this.

> 'The fact is, we have all been a good deal puzzled because the affair is so simple, and yet baffles us altogether.'
> 'Perhaps it is the very simplicity of the thing which puts you at fault,' said my friend.
> 'What nonsense you *do* talk!' replied the Prefect, laughing heartily.
> 'Perhaps the mystery is a little *too* plain,' said Dupin.
> 'Oh, good heavens! who ever heard of such an idea?'
> 'A little *too* self-evident.'[11]

Could it be that the existence of God is a little too self-evident? We generally do not demand proof of things that are self-evident. Could this be why people like Richard Dawkins consider God to be an absence of an explanation? Is this why, at any cost, the temptation to accept the self-evident as a valid explanation must be resisted? Occasionally, we catch glimpses of this possibility. Francis Crick, co-discoverer of DNA and ardent Darwinist warns that

> "biologists must constantly keep in mind that what they see was not designed, but rather evolved."[12]

This led Phillip Johnson to observe

> "Darwinian biologists must keep repeating that reminder to themselves because otherwise they might become conscious of the reality that is staring them in the face and trying to get their attention."[13]

Surely when we observe 'apparent design', unless we have a very good reason not to interpret the evidence in this way, the most natural explanation for our observation is actual design. As Norman Geisler puts it though, "Dawkins refuses to allow observation to interfere with his conclusions,"[14] because as we have seen already, a materialist conclusion is presupposed even before any observation is made.

What it comes down to is this. If God is so self-evident, let's just presuppose him out of existence, if we can't get rid of him any other way. Let's say that what we want is an 'explanation', but let's define the word 'explanation' to mean 'materialistic explanation'. This way we will be protected from any theistic conclusions and all of the evidence for God's existence will be literally hidden in plain view.

The Masked Magicians

The Devil is like a magician. In a short story called *The Generous Gambler*, the French poet Charles Baudelaire said that the Devil's greatest trick was convincing the world that he didn't exist. Now it would seem that many people have also been convinced that God doesn't exist.

Many people get annoyed by magic tricks, because magicians stubbornly refuse to explain how the tricks are done. Several years ago, professional magicians got very annoyed by a series of television programmes featuring a 'masked magician' who broke the 'magician's code' by explaining how all sorts of tricks were done. These shows were very popular because to look for explanations seems to be a part of human nature.

God is also a bit like a magician too. In the Old Testament, a man named Job suffers very badly at the hands of the Devil. God gives him no explanation as to why he allowed this to happen.

On the cover of one of David Blaine's DVDs, he quotes another magician, Joseph Dunninger, as saying

174

"For those who believe, no explanation is necessary. For those who do not, none will suffice."[15]

It took me a long time to understand what the first line of that might mean. At first it sounds similar to something Richard Dawkins might say; that true believers do not look for explanations but simply settle for a sort of blind faith. This may be what Joseph Dunninger meant when he said it. I believe though that it can be taken in quite a different way. Magic tricks by their very nature require an explanation, but what God does is not a magic trick. For Christians no explanation is necessary because the explanation is not given by the magician; the explanation *is* the magician. God requires no explanation, and things like this infuriate people like Richard Dawkins. The quotation that David Blaine attributes to Joseph Dunninger is actually from Thomas Aquinas, although it is usually rendered, "To one who has faith, no explanation is necessary. To one without faith, no explanation is possible." Aquinas was right because what God is and what God does cannot be explained. They can only be revealed.

Revelation

We have seen throughout this book that your attitude to how you know things is closely related to your beliefs about God. We have also seen Richard Dawkins say that revelation (by which I mean the idea that God can supernaturally disclose knowledge to you directly) is not a good reason for believing something. Obviously Richard Dawkins doesn't believe in divine revelation because he doesn't believe in God, but hopefully you can see that logically, when it comes to revelation and atheism, it is the atheism that comes first. It goes without saying that people could mistakenly believe that they have received a revelation, when in reality they have just made something up, but it does not then follow that the whole idea of divine revelation is false. Just because some insane people hear voices in their head doesn't mean that people do not really talk to each other.

Unfortunately for people like Richard Dawkins, revelation seems to be God's main way of communicating with human beings. As far as the scientific method is concerned, God doesn't seem to appreciate being investigated in that kind of way – I believe that this is what he means when he says in the Bible that we should not put him to the test. God isn't just another part of the universe to be poked and prodded. He is the Creator.

There is a sense in which for scientists to look at the world and say that there is no evidence for the existence of God is similar to Sherlock Holmes carrying out a thorough investigation only to come to the conclusion that there is no evidence for the existence of Sir Arthur Conan Doyle. God is not a part of his creation. If you believe that Sherlock Holmes would have been right to conclude that there was no evidence to be found for the existence of Sir Arthur Conan Doyle you may well be correct, but Sir Arthur Conan Doyle did actually exist. Now is that fair? Could you blame Sherlock Holmes? Surely, for Holmes to believe in his creator, Conan Doyle would have needed to have revealed himself somehow.

Now this is where it gets interesting. One of the ways in which Sir Arthur Conan Doyle could have revealed himself to Sherlock Holmes would have been to have written himself into his own stories as a character. In this way he would have made himself visible and detectable to his detective. Conan Doyle, however, never did write himself into his own stories but another writer of detective fiction, Agatha Christie, did. Several times she wrote herself into her own stories as a character named Ariadne Oliver. Would Hercule Poirot have been correct in concluding that there was no evidence for the existence of Agatha Christie? Hercule Poirot did meet Ariadne Oliver but he never seemed to realise that he was, in a sense, actually meeting his creator. How could the character Ariadne Oliver, if she had known who she really was, have proved to Poirot that she was in fact Agatha Christie; the woman who at that very moment was giving him life and allowing him to carry out the very investigation that may result in the conclusion that she herself did not exist? It's an interesting question.

Now, as it happens, Agatha Christie only ever introduced the character of Ariadne Oliver as a sort of joke, but God claims to have entered into this world and revealed himself to his creatures on countless occasions. The most significant of these revelations, the Bible claims, occurred when God himself was born at a real time in a real place and as a real person named Jesus. Even then most of the people who met Jesus did not know that they were meeting their Creator. Even the disciples did not work it out by themselves. This knowledge had to be revealed. In Matthew's gospel, chapter 16, Jesus asks Peter the disciple, "Who do you say I am?" Peter replies, "You are the Christ, the Son of the living God," and Jesus replies, "Blessed are you, Simon son of Jonah, for this was not revealed to you by man, but by my Father in heaven."

So what more do you want God to do? And surely if God is who he says he is, what does it matter what you want him to do? You are in no position to make demands. Did God say to Job, "The reason you had to suffer was because some people badly need to be ill for their own sake, and some people badly need to be ill to provide important choices for others"? No. Only a world populated by people who believe that they have a 'right' to an 'explanation' for everything would even dream of resorting to such a crass statement as that.

This is not to say that searching for explanations is a bad thing in itself. I believe that God is very much in favour of science. It's just that we can get to a point where we are in danger of overstepping the mark and God simply says to us, as he said to Job, "Where were you when I laid the foundations of the earth?"[16] In other words, God puts us in our place. We are not God. We are merely his creatures. In the Bible, God says that we will find him when we search for him with all our hearts. He does not say that we will find him when we search for him with the correct scientific experiment, and the problem is that if scientific experiments are all that you've got or all that you trust, then you probably won't end up becoming a Christian.

The Final Problem

By stripping life of its spiritual dimension, people like Richard Dawkins have lost the ability to submit to God's reality. All that is left is a pseudo-explanation. Of course, the magician does not spell it out for us; we have to discover it for ourselves. Intellectual pride is a wonderfully useful device, as people like Derren Brown know all too well. The actual pseudo-explanation could be anything that sounds even remotely plausible enough to explain how the world could have come into existence without God. This view of the world will obviously be a reductionist one, but what does it matter if we get rid of superfluous concepts such as 'meaning'? Natural selection will do as well as any other pseudo-explanation for 'the whole of life'. There may even be some truth in it. Remember how mixing a little bit of truth in with the lies only helps to strengthen the overall effect. If a theory can explain *some things*, pretend it can explain *everything*. If a theory *could* be true, conclude that it *must* be true. Just add a bit of 'magic circularity' to ignore any evidence that doesn't seem to fit, and where there are gaps in the explanation such as where the first life came from – well, just because we don't know *everything* now, that doesn't mean we won't discover it one day. Surely it would be arrogant to believe that we knew everything. Wouldn't it?

If life really is like a detective story, then on our own we don't stand a very good chance of coming up with the correct solution. However, since becoming a Christian I have discovered something that I never expected; the answers provided in the Bible are like the final chapter of the detective story in which everything is explained and, as the Van Dine Principle says, once you allow these ideas to sink in and look

178

at the world from this new perspective, *everything* seems to point to the truth of Christianity and you can't help but wonder why you never saw it before. C. S. Lewis famously said,

> "I believe in Christianity as I believe that the sun has risen: not only because I see it, but because by it I see everything else."[16]

I know exactly what he means because I experience this feeling every day. When you become a Christian it is as though everything is suddenly different and nothing is what you thought it was. It really is a different world.

In the end I am either right or I am wrong. If I am wrong then I am a deluded, unreliable narrator, and this book of mine is just a trick. But the thing is, if I am right, and you are an atheist, then you will still think that I am wrong. Even now, your presuppositions will be determining how you interpret the evidence, and if I am actually right, and it is you who are deluded, then quite possibly you are caught in the ultimate thinking trap, and unless God reveals himself to you somehow, you will be perfectly happy to stay there, safe in the knowledge that you have successfully avoided being manipulated by a crazy, religious fanatic.

So this leaves me more than a little confused by the slightly odd collection of quotes on the back cover of *The God Delusion*. We have one of the most successful children's authors of recent years, Philip Pullman, and psychologist Steven Pinker both calling the book elegant, when it most certainly isn't elegant; in fact, I doubt that Dawkins ever intended it to be elegant. On the whole, it has to be said that *The God Delusion* is rather an aggressive book. Then we have Derren Brown saying that this book is his favourite book of all time. I'm almost tempted to say that I simply don't believe him!

I still think Derren Brown is great, and I would even go as far as to say that I quite like Richard Dawkins too. As horrendously mistaken as I believe Dawkins to be, I do agree with Derren Brown when he says that *The God Delusion* is a courageous book. As a Christian though, I feel that it is our duty to stand up against works such as this and attempt to be equally courageous. It is not unreasonable to be a Christian. Not all faith is blind faith. Christians should not, when asked why they do not attempt to defend Christianity using rational arguments, say "I never knew I could," and if that doesn't make us unpopular enough, no matter how much Richard Dawkins would hate us for it, and no matter how patronising Derren Brown would consider it to be, we have no alternative but to continue to pray for them both.

Notes

Chapter 1: Introduction

1. John Lloyd and John Mitchinson, *The Book of General Ignorance.* London: Faber and Faber, 2006, page xiii

2. Ibid.

3. Comedian Ricky Gervais includes several references to his own atheism in his stand-up comedy, for example on the *Animals* DVD. He also expressed his opinions regarding God's non-existence through the character of Andy Millman, in the Kate Winslett episode of his sitcom *Extras*.

4. This can be found in the article *Atheists for Jesus* written by Richard Dawkins on his personal website www.richarddawkins.net, where he can be seen wearing his 'Atheists for Jesus' T-shirt that he refers to in the book *The God Delusion*.

5. These are Derren Brown's two previous books, *Pure Effect* and *Absolute Magic*, that were written for magicians but are now easily available, courtesy of the Internet, to anybody who wants to read them. They are both great books, if you're interested in magic, and I recommend them both wholeheartedly.

6. According to Derren Brown, in an interview with Jamy Ian Swiss for the February 2005 edition of *Genii Magazine*, the term 'psychological illusionist' was made up by a TV listings magazine. A transcript of this very interesting interview can be found at http://www.jamyianswiss.com/fm/works/derren-brown.html

7. Richard Dawkins, *The God Delusion*. London: Bantam, 2006, page 5

8. *The God Delusion*, page 37

9. This was part of an interview between Robert Winston and Ken Ham, included in the final part of the BBC television series *The Story of God.* (2005)

10. This was during an episode of *The Heaven and Earth Show* (2006) where Steve Jones was being interviewed about a lecture he was to give to the Royal Society explaining 'why creationism is wrong and evolution is right'. The figure of 44% referred to the percentage of the British population who thought that creationism should be taught in school science lessons alongside Darwinian evolution.

11. Ken Ham and Paul Taylor, *The Genesis Solution.* Michigan: Baker Book House, 1988, page 17

12. Stephen Fry, *Moab is my Washpot: An Autobiography*. New York: Random House, 1999, page 16

13. This was at the official launching of the Church of England's 2004-05 series of Alpha Courses in Birmingham. Sadly, Pete McCahon died in December 2004 of a heart attack.

14. If you are not familiar with *The Screwtape Letters*, it is a book of letters from a senior demon (named Screwtape) to a junior demon (named

Wormwood), where Screwtape gives Wormwood advice on how to handle a human being he has been put in charge of. In my opinion, it is possibly the best of all C. S. Lewis's books.

Chapter 2: Pre-Show Work

1. Derek Acorah was allegedly exposed as a fraud by the makers of the television programme *Most Haunted*. Various names such as 'Kreed Kafer' (an anagram of 'Derek faker') and 'Rik Eedles' (an anagram of 'Derek lies') were mentioned by crew members before the recording of an episode. Acorah then claimed to be in contact with these fictional characters and, in one case, even possessed by one of them. Yvette Fielding, who hosts the show, was quoted as saying that Derek Acorah was dropped from the programme because he was "a fake".

2. I do not mention it here as it is not really relevant, but there is a third way of interpreting the diagram. Anybody from a culture not accustomed to representing three dimensional images in two dimensions would probably just see the diagram as a collection of lines and not as any kind of cube at all.

3. A.F. Chalmers, *What is this thing called Science? (Second Edition)*. Milton Keynes: Open University Press, 1982, page 26

4. This is something that Ken Ham often says when giving lectures on creation vs. evolution.

5. Derren Brown, *Pure Effect*. Texas: H&R Magic Books, Third Edition, 2000, page 102

6. *The God Delusion*, page 104

7. Blaise Pascal, *The Art of Persuasion*.

8. Quoted in the article *Why We Want To Believe Psychics* on the BBC website, dated Wednesday 22nd September 2004, Professor Richard Wiseman holds Britain's only chair in the Public Understanding of Psychology at the University of Hertfordshire.

9. I am here referring to Dawkins' statement that the universe has 'no design, no purpose, no evil and no good, nothing but blind pitiless indifference.' This can be found in his book *River out of Eden: A Darwinian View of Life*. London: Phoenix, 1995, page 133.

10. *The God Delusion*, page 232

11. *The God Delusion*, page 216

12. *The God Delusion*, page 116

13. *The God Delusion*, page 188

14. C. S. Lewis, *The Problem of Pain*. London: Geoffrey Bles, 1940, chapter 8

15. I am not here suggesting that this is how Derren Brown performs this effect.

16. Phillip E. Johnson, *Defeating Darwinism by Opening Minds*. Illinois: InterVarsity Press, 1997, page 21. Phillip E. Johnson is best known as the author of the classic book *Darwin on Trial*, first published in 1991.

17. *The God Delusion*, page 36
18. From an e-mail sent from Richard Dawkins to Phillip E. Johnson on July 10, 2001. The entire exchange can be found at http://www.arn.org/docs/pjweekly/pj_weekly_010813.htm
19. Richard Feynman, *The Value of Science* (speech at NAS meeting, 1955) reprinted in *The Pleasure of Finding Things Out: The Best Short Works of Richard P. Feynman*, Jeffrey Robbins, ed., 1999
20. Richard Dawkins is not unaware of this problem. He mentions it in a quotation on page 371 of *The God Delusion*. He offers no explanation, however, of how this continuity might be maintained.

Chapter 3: Tricks of the Mind

1. Andy Nyman, Derren Brown's co-writer on his television series, has a card routine called *Charade* on his excellent *Get Nyman* DVD which utilises this principle.
(*Get Nyman* DVD is available from http://www.alakazam.co.uk)
2. Using a 'key card' is when you know the name of the card next to a spectator's card. You can then find their card by finding the card next to your key card.
3. Derren Brown, *Tricks of the Mind*. London: Channel 4 Books, 2006. If you have a copy of this book you can read his reasons for giving up Christianity in full on pages 5 to 16.
4. *Tricks of the Mind*, page 15
5. *Tricks of the Mind*, page 12
6. C. S. Lewis, *Surprised by Joy*, London: Geoffrey Bles, 1955, page 215
7. I took this quotation from page 64 of dc Talk's *Jesus Freaks*. (Eagle Publishing, 2000) but the original source of the quotation can be found in the preface to Richard Wurmbrand's *Sermons in Solitary Confinement*, (London: Hodder and Stoughton, 1969) which is an excellent book.
8. Alister McGrath, *Dawkins' God: Genes, Memes and the Meaning of Life*. Oxford: Blackwell, 2004, page 88.
9. *Tricks of the Mind*, page 15
10. *Tricks of the Mind*, page 13
11. *Tricks of the Mind*, page 12
12. *Tricks of the Mind*, page 13
13. *The God Delusion*, page 50
14. *Tricks of the Mind*, page 14
15. *Tricks of the Mind*, page 15
16. Ravi Zacharias, *The Real Face of Atheism* Michigan: Baker Books, 2004, pages 174-175
17. *The God Delusion*, page 59
18. *Tricks of the Mind*, page 14
19. *Tricks of the Mind*, page 7
20. *The God Delusion*, page 31
21. Richard Dawkins, *The Blind Watchmaker*. Harlow: Longman, 1986

22. There have been a number of books on this subject, one of the most recent being *The Goldilocks Enigma* by Paul Davies (2006).

23. Romans 1:17-18

24. Bertrand Russell, "Is There a God?", 1952.

25. *Tricks of the Mind*, page 12

26. Richard Dawkins, *The Blind Watchmaker*.

27. *The God Delusion*, page 59

28. Hugh Laurie, *The Gun Seller*. London, William Heinemann Ltd, 1996, page 205.

29. The Velvet Turnover is a card sleight invented by Derren Brown. It is described in detail in his book *Pure Effect*.

30. *The God Delusion*, page 31

Chapter 4: Sleight of Mind

1. Agatha Christie was accused at the time, by various reviewers, of cheating. She mentions this in her autobiography (*An Autobiography*, Harper Collins Publishers, 1977, pages 352-353)

2. Derren Brown and Andy Nyman discuss the issue of context briefly on the DVD commentary to episode 1 of series 2 of the Derren's television series *Trick of the Mind*, during the 'Seeing through Fingertips #1' sequence.

3. for example, on pages 56 and 57 of *The God Delusion*.

4. The 'ideomotor suggestion' or 'ideomotor movement' is the name given to the principle that says that if you think of an object you will, very slightly, physically move towards the thing you are thinking about, and similarly if you think about making a movement, you will, very slightly, make the movement you are thinking of. This can be put to great magical effect, and Derren Brown describes it in *Tricks of the Mind* on pages 45 and 46.

5. *The God Delusion*, page 77

6. *The God Delusion*, page 80

7. Richard Dawkins, *A Devil's Chaplain: Selected Essays*. London: Weidenfeld & Nicolson, 2003

8. *Tricks of the Mind*, page 19

9. *Tricks of the Mind*, page 21

10. *Tricks of the Mind*, page 217

11. Episodes of the first series of Derren Brown's *Trick of the Mind* opened and closed with a passer by picking up a ringing public telephone, only to collapse to the ground moments later, having fallen asleep.

12. Derren Brown, *Absolute Magic*. Texas: H&R Magic Books, Second Edition, pages 62 and 63

13. Debate between Richard Dawkins and Steven Pinker at Westminster Central Hall, London, on 19th February 1999, chaired by Tim Radford, science correspondent of the *Guardian*.

14. Alister McGrath, *Dawkins' God*, page 87

15. *Tricks of the Mind*, page 264
16. Derren Brown, *Pure Effect*, page 32
17. Richard Dawkins, *The Selfish Gene*. Oxford: Oxford University Press, page 198
18. Richard Dawkins, *The Selfish Gene*, page 330
19. Alister McGrath, *Dawkins' God*, page 91
20. Ibid.
21. Carl Sagan, *Cosmos*. New York: Random House, 1980, page 4
22. *The God Delusion*, page 51
23. *The God Delusion*, page 37
24. *The God Delusion*, page 36
25. *The God Delusion*, page 31
26. Andy Nyman is another great magician – the instance I am referring to occurs during his routine *Deep Red Prediction* from his *Get Nyman* DVD (available from www.alakazam.co.uk) but is more explicit on *The Andy Nyman Lecture* (available from International Magic.)
27. Robert M. Pirsig, *Zen and the Art of Motorcycle Maintenance*. first published in Great Britain by The Bodley Head, 1974.
28. Richard Dawkins, *A Devil's Chaplain*, page 257
29. G. K. Chesterton was a Roman Catholic writer from the late nineteenth and early twentieth century. He wrote many Christian books, the most famous of which are probably *Orthodoxy* (1908), *The Everlasting Man* (1925) and his biographies of Thomas Aquinas (1923) and Saint Francis of Assisi (1933). He was, along with George MacDonald, a great influence on C. S. Lewis.
30. George Carlin is an American stand-up comedian.
31. *Tricks of the Mind*, page 192
32. This is from episode one of Richard Dawkins' two part television programme *Root of All Evil?*
33. *The God Delusion*, page 58
34. *The God Delusion*, page 47
35. The Sherlock Holmes story referred to here is *The Red Headed League*. Conan Doyle offers no translation of the Latin in his original short story, but when it was adapted for television (in the excellent series from the 1980s with Jeremy Brett playing Holmes), Dr. Watson translates the phrase as 'everything becomes commonplace by explanation'. Holmes says that this translation is 'loose'.
36. *The God Delusion*, page 11
37. Richard Dawkins, *The Blind Watchmaker*, page xiii
38. Ibid.
39. *Tricks of the Mind*, page 11
40. Ravi Zacharias, *The Real Face of Atheism*. Michigan: Baker Books, 2004, page 25
41. Alister McGrath, *Dawkins' God*, page 113
42. Ibid.
43. Darrell Huff, *How to Lie with Statistics*. London: Victor Gollancz, 1954

44. Alister McGrath with Joanna Collicutt McGrath, *The Dawkins Delusion*. London: SPCK, 2007, page 5

45. *The God Delusion*, page 104

46. *The God Delusion*, page 278

47. J. Gresham Machen, *Christianity and Liberalism*. Michigan: WM. B. Eerdmans Publishing Company, 1923, page 2

48. Richard Dawkins, *River Out of Eden*. London: Weidenfeld & Nicolson, 1995

49. *Tricks of the Mind*, page 13

50. *The God Delusion*, page 55

51. *The God Delusion*, page 57

52. The way Derren Brown describes what he does has changed as his act has evolved and he has become more well-known. In his original *Mind Control* television special he stressed the psychological aspect of his work and claimed that he was not performing magic tricks. As a result, Derren Brown was added to the science section of Channel Four's website, prompting Simon Singh to write a scathing article about him, challenging him to read his mind. This article can be found at http://www.simonsingh.com/Derren_Brown_Article.html

53. Derren Brown says this in *The Derren Brown Lecture*, a video available from International Magic.

54. This 'Taxi' sequence, where the cab driver cannot remember where the London Eye is, even though it is right in front of him, is from episode 1 of series 1 of *Trick of the Mind*.

55. This idea is discussed in *Tricks of the Mind* on pages 132 to 153.

Chapter 5: A Devil's Commentary

1. Andy Warhol, *From A to B & Back Again: The Philosophy of Andy Warhol*. London: Michael Dempsey, 1975, page 77

2. Richard Dawkins does not say where this quotation comes from.

3. "Never judge a philosophy by its abuse" is something that was said by Saint Augustine of Hippo.

4. Richard Dawkins, *River out of Eden*.

5. Oliver Sacks, *Uncle Tungsten: Memories of a Chemical Boyhood*. London: Picador, 2001, page 25

6. Norman L. Geisler and Frank Turek, *I Don't Have Enough Faith to Be an Atheist*. Wheaton, Illinois: Crossway Books, 2004, page 138

7. 1 John 4:1

8. Here I refer to 1 Corinthians 1:26-27

9. Here I am referring to the book of 2 Corinthians. Roy Clements once wrote a book (in 1994) based on 2 Corinthians called *The Strength of Weakness*. In the first chapter he makes the point that the Christian idea of a leader is very different to the idea that the world has. Rather than being strong, in the usual sense of the word, a Christian leader should be somebody who is 'painfully aware of their inadequacies, and their incompetence.'

10. Blaise Pascal, *The Art of Persuasion.*

11. Here I refer to Proverbs 30:8-9

12. Stephen Jay Gould, *Darwinian Fundamentalism.*

13. Douglas Adams is best known as the author of *The Hitchhikers Guide to the Galaxy.*

14. Proverbs 26:4

15. Alister McGrath and Joanna Collicutt McGrath, *The Dawkins Delusion*, page 6

16. Richard Dawkins, *River out of Eden*, page 133

17. 'Relativizing the Relativizers' is the title of chapter 2 of Peter L. Berger's classic book *A Rumour of Angels: Modern Society and the Rediscovery of the Supernatural.* (Penguin Books, 1970)

18. This is a play on "Saul has slain his thousands, and David his tens of thousands" which can be found in 1 Samuel 18:7 and a couple of other places in the book of 1 Samuel.

19. Again, I am referring to the article *Atheists for Jesus*, written by Richard Dawkins that is available to read on his personal website www.richarddawkins.net

20. *The God Delusion*, page 54

Chapter 6: The Greatest Trick?

1. S. S. Van Dine, *The American Magazine*, September 1928, pages 129-131

2. Derren Brown, *Absolute Magic*, page 64

3. This was mentioned in the interview with Jamy Ian Swiss that can be found at http://www.jamyianswiss.com/fm/works/derren-brown.html

4. Derren Brown, *Pure Effect*, page 118

5. *Tricks of the Mind*, page 257

6. Harry Houdini, *Houdini on Magic.* New York: Dover Publications, Inc, 1953, page 123

7. 1 John 4:1

8. A.F. Chalmers, *What is this thing called Science? (Second Edition).* Milton Keynes: Open University Press, 1982, page 28

9. Romans 1:20

10. *Tricks of the Mind*, page 136. The idea of something being hidden in plain view is the idea behind Andy Nyman's trick *Deep Red Prediction*, named after the Italian horror film *Deep Red*, directed by Dario Argento.

11. Edgar Allan Poe's short story *The Purloined Letter* first appeared in *The Gift: A Christmas and New Year's Present for 1844* and was subsequently included in the 1845 collection *Tales by Edgar A. Poe.*

12. Quoted in Phillip E. Johnson, *The Wedge of Truth.* Downers Grove, Illinois: InterVarsity Press, 2000, page 153

13. Phillip E. Johnson, *The Wedge of Truth.*

14. Norman L. Geisler and Frank Turek, *I Don't Have Enough Faith to Be an Atheist.* Wheaton, Illinois: Crossway Books, 2004, page 119

15. This quotation is taken from the front cover of David Blaine's *Mystifier* DVD.

16. Job 38:4

17. C.S. Lewis, "Is Theology Poetry?" *The Weight of Glory and other Addresses.* New York: Harper Collins publishers, 1980, page 140.

Printed in the United Kingdom by
Lightning Source UK Ltd., Milton Keynes
136621UK00001B/43-45/P